DOGdays

DOGdays

Penny Simpson

First impression—2003

ISBN 1 84323 228 6

This book is published with the support of the Arts Council of Wales.

Printed in Wales at
Gomer Press, Llandysul, Ceredigion SA44 4QL

To the memory of my father
Alexander James Simpson
(1924–1997)

Contents

PLAYING THE JOKER

'You should have "I do" printed up on your bastard T-shirt, Clance. Said it that many times and with that many different men, you could save your breath to smoke the ciggies you got stashed.'

Dermot delivered his verdict with a flourish: he flicked a beer mat into the air and watched it perform a near-perfect arc before slipping down Clancy's logo-free chest. She didn't like the idea – had learnt young to avoid attention from unwanted men. Ironic then, that she'd ended up in this line of work. She had the one suit for the registry office. Pastel pink with a matching plastic flower for her hair. The mobile went and she was told the day and time when the job was to be done and off she went, twisting her poppy in her ponytail and rehearsing her lines like an actress poised in the wings.

Clancy bit her fingernails and tried to damp down Dermot's scorn. She didn't get married, not properly. He knew that, so why did he cod on about her 'husbands'? Truth was, she was never curious about any of them. Some hardly spoke English, so it was hard to strike up much in the way of a conversation. Others were anxious, fussing over non-existent paperwork. They were lined up for work in fruit fields, if they were lucky. And if they were unlucky? Clancy didn't ask. If you'd lived on the sites as long as she had, you knew all about the random injustice. Picked on, picked up. Angry protesters emptying rubbish bins on the caravan steps – and worse. *You gonna bastard ruin this place anyways, so we just saving you some time . . .*

The council produced official documents which said the same but in fancy talk. Sean Choke up at the Wentloog site understood them, because he had made a study of the law in prison:

'Can't bastard argue with letters, lovely,' he told Clancy.

'Black and white, see? No muddle.'

She had always understood muddle better than she did the alphabet. And here she was on the eve of Wedding Number Eight and she was still trying to reason with Dermot.

'It's just a job, yeah? So, what's the problem?'

'But have you never wanted to . . . you know . . .'

'That's not what the deal is. I just have to say "I do." They need someone to stand there and go through the motions, that's what Mikhail says.'

'Don't like his cut.'

'He don't like yours, neither.'

Clancy had liked Mikhail straight away though. Short and wiry with bright green eyes; his suit was too big for him, his Caterpillar boots were worn at the heels. He paid her with bank notes wrapped up in glossy magazines.

'Something to read on your wedding night,' he said.

He didn't know she couldn't read. He bought her *Tatler*, *Vogue* and *Harpers & Queen*. Clancy asked Sean to read the picture captions.

'Fuck me, five grand for a coat!'

Clancy liked the party photographs best of all. Smiling guests with pipe-cleaner bodies, wearing clothes that cost more than all of her weddings put together. But it didn't seem to hurt anyone, except in their wallets, maybe. Clancy wished others could cotton on to this idea. As it was, her Wentloog neighbours always joked about her 'weddings.' She tried to keep her transactions quiet, but everyone knew what she was up to the minute she showed in her pink suit and pink slingbacks.

'Making an honest woman of you again, is it!'

Dermot standing back from their loud catcalling. Brow corrugated; hands tucked up under his armpits. His whole body spelling resentment. Clancy was aware of his confusion but was powerless to change it. Since the wedding scam had started, her mind had turned into an alphabet soup that hardly matched Dermot's view of the world.

'Gretna Green is supposed to be *the* place,' Dermot claimed. 'Not for me, mind. I want something more upmarket, yeah? Like a country house with a koi carp pond. You like them, Clance? Sort of posh goldfish, they is.'

'Who you gonna marry then, Dermot?'

'Well, you're spoken for. Dozens of times over. That would be illegal, that would.'

'It's just different names all juggled up. Me Mam's, your Mam's, whoever. I learns the words off by heart, but I don't really *feel* them. Not like when I says things in my own way.'

Dermot remained unconvinced, even after she'd bought him four pints of Brains in a row. Clancy tried another tack:

'We should give those poor buggers a chance of a party at least,' she reflected. 'Year ago today, right, I marries a man who lost all his family. They burnt him in prison. Battery acid. His lips melted together . . .'

But Clancy knew she was getting nowhere with her explanations. They'd been going out for nearly three years, but Dermot was always uneasy when she talked about her on-off job as a bride. It had begun shortly after they'd met. That first wedding was in a stifling registry office in Bethnal Green. A licence, a box of confetti and a *Vogue* magazine full of bank notes, no bridesmaids, or best man – unless you counted Mikhail. Not even flutes of dry champagne. Bride and groom turned up ten minutes before the ceremony started and introduced themselves. The groom spoke enough English to recite the words Mikhail had written down for him on the back of a shop flyer, no more.

They'd stood smiling awkwardly at each other as Mikhail telephoned yet another fixer in the little drama that was unwinding around them. The groom had blue eyes and a suit he had been lent by Mikhail. The sleeves concertinaed up his biceps and the trousers barely touched the tops of his socks. Clancy had on her brand-new pink suit and a gold necklace that had been a present from Dermot.

'It means good luck,' she whispered to her groom. 'We've kept to the tradition. Something old, something new, something borrowed, something blue.'

He hadn't understood the words, but Clancy had no time to explain. They were back outside where Dermot sneaked up on them, shades glued to his face.

'Who is he, Clance? I'll kill the bastard!'

It wasn't till after a flurry of punches and Mikhail biting his flailing hand that Dermot had let the sight of his own blood subdue him. Explanations in the cafe over the road. The stranger in the borrowed suit thinking God knew what; Clancy nursing Dermot's torn palm and pleading:

'The licences are just pretend ones and I get £100 and my travel.'

That had always been the way with them, Clancy thought. Dermot was hot and furious, like a forest fire; she was calm and took her time. Brushed her hair out with fifty strokes each morning and applied her eyeliner as straight as if her life depended on it. She didn't want to understand more than she already did.

The odd revelation dropped by the unknown husbands scared her. She didn't have an alternative script to the one she'd prepared with Mikhail's assistance. *My name is Clancy O'Riordan. I do. Love and cherish. Thank you. Good luck. May the wind always be at your back . . .*

Later, heading for the train back to Cardiff, she had nearly trodden on a baby mouse scuttling through the feet of the London Underground commuters. The thumb-sized mouse was lost, panicking amongst a caravan of moving feet. That's how the strangers must feel, she thought. A confusion of airport lounge, wedding, a safe house, a derelict house. Fruit picking, sweat shop. The choices were few, but how many did a man need before exhaustion swept him down into chaos, like that baby mouse? She'd grown up on the sites and had had little idea that other people's lives could be as miserable as her own. No right to settle anywhere, no running water, no jobs, no money, no respect. A verdict made and delivered – no appeal heeded. And then the chance encounter with Mikhail in a pub off Broadway. A chance to put some money her way. A chance to have an adventure. A chance to say, *I don't love, honour, or obey*.

'Always excuses with you Clance, nothing ever bastard doing.'

Dermot thumped down his pint.

'Why stay in your Da's caravan now he's passed on, an' all? Move in with me. It's not the weddings I mind, see? A scam's a bastard scam, but stalling on me, that's unnatural that is, Clance. Bastard unnatural. Why can't you be like other women?'

She had her excuse ready and waiting: Wedding Number Eight.

'It's going to be a breeze,' Mikhail promised.

'Reading. 11.30am. You meet a guy wearing a leopard-skin hat.'

'As you do,' Clancy replied.

It was a bright June morning. She treated herself to a punnet of peaches from a stall by the railway station. Mangy pigeons and a dreadlocked youth with a day-glo waistcoat emblazoned 'Friends of the Earth' dogged her footsteps. Clancy felt like everyone's friend that morning. She decided she would keep hold of her wedding money, no more 'loans' to Dermot. *What is mine, is yours*, he always said. In truth, it was a one-way traffic that kept her from moving on. There was nothing stopping her from leaving the Wentloog site, if that was her tickle. She was not like the pretend bridegrooms, trapped, relying on someone else to make their world fresh as a Spring crocus for them.

Clancy found Bridegroom Number Eight sitting on the pavement outside the registry office playing a trumpet. She stood on the opposite side of the road and listened to him playing something slow and jazzy. His face crumpled up around the mouthpiece, like a flower not yet ready to bud. He was oblivious to everything else going on around him, intent only on looping the next coil of notes into his melody. Clancy's curiosity was aroused – this was the first of her bridegrooms to have stepped out of the shadows to meet the challenge of the day head on. She crossed the road and planted herself in front of the trumpeter; he finished his music before acknowledging her.

'Hello. I'm Clancy O'Riordan. I'm marrying you at 11.30.'

'Clancy?'

'Yes.'

'I'm Louis.'

His voice was as good to listen to as his trumpet. Reminded her of her Da's voice, which had swooped and curved like a bird's wing. The minute she heard its echo in the stranger, Clancy found herself breaking the rules of her short lifetime as a much-married woman. She sat down next to Louis and asked him about himself.

'I'm from Zimbabwe.'

'Do you play there?'

'Sometimes. In a club, on a street. People always want to hear music, even if they don't want to hear about you.'

Clancy wondered if he might be hungry and offered him one of the peaches.

'The wedding breakfast?'

He gave a smile, which revealed two front teeth that made a shape like a butterfly. Clancy had to resist the urge to tap them with her fingers. Their wedding was

16

delayed by the one in front of them – they watched a gaggle of sailors file in behind a teenage bride and groom. Louis shook his head.

'Everyone in such a rush, Clancy. People should put on the brake. Shake the dust out of their shoes.'

She took him at his word. Pulled off her slingbacks, loosened her hair and prayed that Mikhail would get diverted – arrested even. Let it all come to light. She had a conversation to finish. Louis put down his trumpet and touched her hair.

'Look at me nice,' he asked her.

She smiled at him.

'You really married, Clancy?'

'No.'

'You even with anyone?'

'I'm not sure. You do this for a living, how do you know what is your life anymore? Everything's all shuffled up.'

'Good money?'

'Enough to get me through the gaps.'

Louis frowned. Her accent worried him. He couldn't catch her meaning. His hand was still locked in her hair.

'I don't have any qualifications, see? Not many of us do where I live. We travel a lot. No putting down roots, like a tree does.'

'The man who set this up for me, he says I must take "pot luck." What is this, Clancy?'

'More of the shuffling.'

'Waiting for the aces?'

'Could be.'

'You can be my Queen of Diamonds and I shall be the Joker in the pack. What else can I be? I stop laughing, who knows?'

'Then stay laughing, Louis.'

Clancy dug her toes down on sun-hot paving stones, her fingers wet with peach juice. Louis produced a handkerchief from a pocket – bright red with a gold signature embroidered in a corner.

'Gift from a man with no loose change.'

'I'll make it all messy. You might not get a chance to wash it later.'

Clancy blushed. Louis shrugged, as if to say there was no knowing what lay ahead so why worry about a handkerchief? He was magnificently self-contained at that moment. No rants, or tears, or even blows. He wore the challenge of his new life as he would a mohair suit. He would make it fit into his way of being, just as he did his trumpet's notes. Louis took another peach. He ate it slowly, taking small bites and licking up the juice as he went.

'Now you,' he said, holding up the half-eaten fruit.

When she finished eating, he plucked the stone from out of her mouth.

'Maybe you could work as a musician, Louis?'

'Not in the plan.'

'What plan?'

Clancy felt anxious. She remembered Mikhail

muttering about people crushed under pallets of rotting fruit. Bones folded up and cutting into their bellies like knives.

'The plan they give you when you pay up the money. I owe a lot of money.'

'How come?'

'You think I fly over here with the birds? There's always a price to pay, Clancy. Even this old corpse has a price. But look, I've met you.'

'I'm only pretend, Louis. And I'm paid to do this.'

'Sure. You are what I want you to be. It's a deal, yes?'

'I'm the Queen of Diamonds?'

'I'm marrying into royalty. It will impress them back home.'

'Will they ever know?'

'One day, perhaps.'

Clancy was grateful to Louis all of a sudden. Usually, she gave legitimacy to someone else by signing away one of her made-up names. Today, she knew it was different. She could add little more to this man's life – he had everything he most needed when he played his music. And when he talked to her, he made her feel that she was his equal. No catch-out questions or drunken rows. Clancy walked into the registry office, electric with anticipation.

'Your shoes, Clancy. You going to wear your shoes?'

She turned round. Louis stood outside, his trumpet held up in one hand, her shoes in the other. Clancy strapped them back on her feet in the reception area where the registrar, a tiny woman in a ruby red suit, bounced up to welcome them.

'Don't you two look a picture!' she exclaimed, hurrying them into the adjoining room where Mikhail stood, a copy of *Vogue* rolled up in his coat pocket.

'I don't think I'll be needing a magazine tonight,' Clancy whispered in his ear.

Mikhail started, but she moved on. Louis sat on the table where the registrar hovered. Seeing her approach, he put his trumpet to his lips and broke into the wedding march.

ATGOFION (REMEMBRANCES)

Nadja played with the beads on her wrist. The man opposite her was getting impatient. She read it in his face each time she dared to look him in the eye. He couldn't make the tape recorder work, he had burnt his lip on his coffee – even his tie betrayed him. There were spots of something red and hard on its pale yellow design. Blood?

Nadja twisted the little silver beads faster and faster. The question the man had just asked her hung in the air alongside the curl of cigarette smoke he had blown out through his scalded lips. She stared at the photograph he had placed on the table. It was a black and white photograph of Nadja sitting next to a man in a leather jacket. The picture had been taken by her interrogator while 'on surveillance.' Nadja struggled with the English words. She tried to remember the newspaper reports she read in the library where she went to improve her language skills. 'Surveillance.' It meant someone was being watched by somebody else. She was being watched by another man who stood at a distance from the table. He listened to everything she said, but he didn't speak.

'So, yesterday was the first time you meet Mestrovic?'

'Slow, please.'

Nadja had already told them twice, maybe three times, how she had met the man in the photograph. She really had no idea who he was, or what he was, other than he was a man who spoke the language of her heart. The truth circled Nadja's head, like a waltzer. Had she repeated Mestrovic's exact words? If she managed that, maybe they would let her go home? Yesterday, she had been sitting at a different table in a cafe close to her hostel and another stranger had been asking her questions. Nadja was quietly crying behind a newspaper. The stranger offered her a napkin from the dispensary on the cafe counter and then sat down opposite her. She blew her nose and muttered her gratitude in broken English. He had picked up on her accent immediately. He knew who she was even though she sat thousands of miles from her home and gave no personal information about herself. He knew why she cried alone in a cafe. He knew many people like her, he said, too many people. He even spoke a little of her language, which Nadja seriously thought she might never hear again. She clapped her hands, as if he had just performed a complicated aria for her.

'Temporary, or long stay?'

'I don't know yet. I make an application. I wait.'

'Ah, you wait also. The cafes in this city are full of people who wait.'

At least she could sit down and warm her hands on a cup of coffee. Nadja had waited in queues that crossed fluid borders and unmapped mountain passes. Once, a woman had even given birth in the crowd that pressed in around her, relying on a stranger to catch her falling baby, slippery with blood and blue as a cornflower. By the time they reached the soldiers standing around a card table, the baby had died. Nadja suspected the stranger knew her story already; if not this exact story, one with similar contours. She had told nobody since going into exile, she explained, not even the immigration people. She was afraid she might speak the wrong words, her story would be misunderstood and she would be sent to prison.

'My name is Zoran,' the stranger introduced himself. 'My paper work for the authorities is already completed. How is this? It is because I know people who know the short cuts.'

He lit a cigarette for Nadja and smiled the smile she remembered from the men sitting in the cafe where she used to work. They dressed in uniforms of their own devising. Nadja had learnt to balance their steaming cups of black coffee on a beaten silver tray when the mortar shells fell close by. Zoran shook his head, a big bear's head topped with shaggy, badly-dyed blond hair. His leather jacket was new and shiny and matched his loafers.

'You can break the rules, Nadja, of course you can. You will have learnt how to live without them long before you moved into exile. Some of my friends in the army were Roma people. I know how it was with them.'

Zoran didn't specify which army and Nadja knew not to ask him – her people had often been denounced as collaborators by all sides. In one of the border camps, a Roma boy had been nearly torn apart by the other refugees. A woman standing close to Nadja claimed to recognise the necklace he was wearing. It was her necklace, she insisted, he must have stolen it. Her friends screeched judgement on the boy, ripping at his face with their fingers. The soldiers on duty plucked him up, like a broken animal, firing above the crowd's roaring heads. Sure, Nadja could live without rules, but not without fear.

The man spoke to her in broken sentences from several different languages. He spoke like the women in the border camp who came from places she had never heard of, let alone visited. Everyone spoke a babel of languages, anxious to find just a few words of comfort they could share in the long hours of queuing. Nadja learnt to mimic an accent that was not her own. The words of her heart soldered themselves to her tongue, as she forced out strange new patterns of meaning that gave her the right piece of paper to keep her moving across the mountains, across water, to arrive in a place of refuge.

'Sanctuary, please.'

They were her first words on foreign soil. The

immigration official smiled, briefly, but he had no time to waste on pleasantries. There was no one who could understand her, not until a translator chanced by the desk where she sat, wordless, in tears. The official was impatient, just like the detective in the interrogation room. He was impatient. Because he was tired, because he was bored, who could tell? The translator helped her case along, but Nadja was scared she would slip up if asked to repeat her testimony. The translator might have said the wrong things, misunderstood her. Nadja knew that one step out of line could ruin her chances of achieving sanctuary. She suddenly envied the baby in its muddy grave and wept at the perversity of her strange desire. Eighteen months later, and here she sat in another room with another persistent interrogator.

'So, Mestrovic didn't offer you anything?' asked the man with the yellow tie, tipping his chair back and staring up at the ceiling as he did so.

'He see me cry and he speak to me, sir. Just a few words really. I have not spoken like this to anyone for . . . for . . . too long, I think. This is what he offer me.'

The detective pulled off his stained yellow tie. He rolled his eyes at his colleague, propped up by the door.

'So, the man's a saint. What do you know about Adam Gazic?'

'Nothing.'

'He didn't show up, did he?'

'I do not understand.'

'He was supposed to be at the meeting with Mestrovic. That was what we heard, lovely.'

'I still don't understand.'

'Look, it's getting late, Nadja, and we seem to be walking round Robin Hood's barn on this one. I've got a home to go to.'

Nadja understood the word 'home.' She stopped playing with her bracelet.

'I go home.'

'Sorry, you won't be going anywhere until you tell us about Mestrovic.'

'I tell you that already, so many times!'

'You're in a cafe, crying. He turns up and offers solidarity over a tissue.'

The silent man burst out laughing. Nadja blushed. She felt cornered, but she had no idea what the rules might be in this odd conversation she had been dragged into by the two policemen. They didn't wear uniforms. They didn't even carry guns. How did she know they were genuine? She wished then she had spoken to Zoran a little longer. He had some understanding of this country's rules and regulations. Nadja tried again:

'Please, I have papers. The hostel knows me.'

'You might not be a criminal, or rather we can't prove you are – yet; but Mestrovic certainly is. A people smuggler, sweetheart. Do you understand that?'

Nadja didn't know what to say. Her mind raced with explanations she could not repeat, because the detectives would not understand. Nadja pulled a bead off her bracelet and listened to it as it spun across the floor.

'Check her in to her room, Gareth.'

Her interrogator wrapped his tie around his balled fist and walked out of the room. Gareth put his hand on Nadja's shoulder and panic took over her shocked senses. She fell to the floor, rolling and twisting like the silver bead. Gareth called out and soon the room was full of people. They pulled her to her feet and shouted into her face. Nadja remembered the boy in the camp. She waited for them to break her limbs and tear out her hair. The noise gradually subsided. A police-woman put her arm round her shoulders.

'Follow me, Nadja. It's okay, lovely.'

Nadja trusted the tone of the woman's voice. She let herself be led up a corridor and into a cell. It was covered in graffiti, like the bus-stop near her hostel. Nadja had no idea what else to do, but walk in and sit down on a solitary bench. Hadn't she learnt to survive in many different places by making herself invisible and very small? Nadja pulled her legs up to her chin and wrapped her arms around her knees. She knew how to wait. She had practically boasted of this skill to Zoran. If she waited long enough, someone might listen to her, just as he had. They might even understand that it was the loss of words that made her so brittle.

Before leaving her country, Nadja had watched gunners target the city's university buildings. She stood in the street outside the cafe where she worked and caught dozens of sheets of burning paper falling from the sky. She burnt her hands on the words of the past, struggling to read them, before they turned to ash. Others joined her. They put out the fires with their fists and feet, wrapped the smouldering fragments in their clothes, tore off a shirt or a jacket to protect the threatened words. One young man burst into tears when he understood what was burning in the sky above him.

'It is our history!' he screamed out to anyone who would listen.

He removed his jumper and his shirt. People stopped and stared as more pages fell to dust against his naked back. Nadja kept running to catch more of the paper snow. The stranger's grief was contagious. When they could gather up no more words, she led him back to her cafe and offered him coffee.

'I'm mad, that's what you think, but people give their life's blood for a lot less,' the young man told her. 'Pride and prejudice, yes? They fall in their graves, but for words like these, they turn away. They are happy to stay ignorant.'

Nadja inspected her fingers, as he spoke. They were still covered in the charred words.

'I will always remember,' she promised him. 'Even when I am no longer able to speak of such things.'

Much to her surprise, Nadja had slept in her cell. The policewoman she had seen the previous day came to wake her up. She was free to go – there were to be no charges to be brought against her. Nadja heard the word 'home' and burst into tears.

'Your friend is waiting, Nadja,' the policewoman said.

Friend? Nadja had been careful to keep herself to herself in the hostel. She didn't trust the men who flanked the stairwells, coats carefully arranged across their shoulders hiding their business from prying eyes. They dealt in food vouchers and tobacco, sometimes the glint of a necklace, or a ring. Nadja's air of self-possession was her only commodity. She used it to buy herself invisibility from the traders. So who could this friend be? She was led out to the desk sergeant who returned her belt, her boot laces and her broken bracelet. A man stood by the desk, smiling at her. He had a greying crew cut and was wearing a green leather blouson jacket. Nadja had never seen him before in her life, but she recognised him all the same.

'Okey, dokey, Nadja?'

An arm was wrapped round her shoulders in a proprietorial gesture. She smelt the piney scent of a cheap aftershave. He whispered to her in her language.

'I'm a friend of Zoran. My name is Darko. We'll get breakfast and talk?'

So that was it. He wasn't her friend, at all. Nadja's stomach rumbled as if on cue. Darko raised his eyebrows at the desk sergeant.

'Grilled kidneys off the menu, man?'

The desk sergeant ignored him, which gave Darko

the opportunity to steer Nadja out of the door. He took her to a café that was too hard on her eyes: all chrome and shining metal fixtures. The ceiling was festooned with sharks and angel fish made out of what appeared to be dented car doors. The garage music beat loud in her head and drowned out Darko's quips to the waitress. She had dirty fingernails and multiple facial piercings, which Nadja assumed had been done to match the metallic interior where she worked. After completing their order, Darko took a comb out of his pocket and combed Nadja's hair. The sudden intimacy of his gesture upset her. She burst into tears all over again.

'It's okay now, Nadja,' Darko said. 'No worries. I make you look like a catwalk model, yes? Look, we can help you. No more tears. No more prison. It's easy peasey, lemon squeezy.'

The last sentence in English made Nadja smile. Nonsense talk – she coped with that in a minute.

'But I have no money.'

'No problem. It's Zoran's treat. Remember him?'

'Yes. He was kind to me.'

'So why do people fail to be kind to him in return? A surprise when you consider how the English always claim one good turn deserves another. You hear this phrase? Could be Zoran's philosophy of life. He wants to do you a good turn – he promised me – and so, of course, he wants something back.'

Darko paused while the waitress set down their two espressos. Nadja felt her hungry stomach twist up with a new emotion: panic. She wondered if she should refuse the breakfast, or confess to Darko what the policemen had told her about his friend's illegal activities during her interrogation? 'You are being watched,' she could say. Was this enough to cover the cost of a full English breakfast? Darko sipped his espresso. His eyelashes were long, like a cow's.

'You are being watched,' she said.

Darko looked up. He understood her meaning. Everyone who was like them understood that no sentence could be complete without a hidden meaning slipped between the words like a very special kind of credit card.

'We know, Nadja. There was a betrayal. Zoran is angry, but nothing more. It's all been sorted out. Damage limitation, you see. We are good at that. We are good at many things. You should trust us.'

Nadja sat back in her metal chair. Now, it was coming. She held herself very still, tried not to let him see her shaking hands.

'Will you trust us? I think you will, because you know what is good for you. I've been watching you, as it happens. I've been watching the detectives watching you watching us! Okey, dokey. You know what they say about Zoran?'

'He is a people smuggler.'

'He is much more than that, baby. Look, you just spent how many months chasing up how many pieces of paper? And the result? You live in a filthy pig sty and you nearly starve. Zoran says you can have better,

31

so believe me, you should go for it. Who else going to provide for you in this hell hole? The immigration people? Nadja, you've seen how they operate. The police? Didn't even get you a cup of tea for your trouble yesterday.'

'What do you want me to do?'

'That's good, Nadja. I like the fact you ask questions. It shows you are thinking ahead. Here's the deal: we can give you a job. We need someone who is prepared to use their eyes on our behalf, yeah?'

'Just my eyes?'

Nadja was surprised by Darko's request. It was not what she had been expecting. He laughed at her incredulity – or was it her naiveté?

'We need someone to watch over us, just like in those bloody hymns we used to sing at school. Remember them? We need someone to act as a lookout. Someone who can blend in, not stand out. Someone who can get rid of the cops. Understand?'

He made it sound non-threatening, nothing more than a scene from one of the films Nadja used to watch in the cinemas at home. Men in trench coats, breathing out plumes of cigarette smoke under the light of a filigree lamp-post.

'That's all?'

Darko smiled. His breath smelt of the thick black coffee he had just drunk.

'That's all, Nadja.'

'I get paid? Proper money?'

'Proper money. And we can get you moved to your own place. A real address and everything brand new.'

'What if it goes wrong?'

'You make sure it doesn't.'

Darko was smiling. His air of confidence was infectious and Nadja felt a wave of optimism fill her – either that or the coffee was playing havoc in her veins. Maybe it was simpler than that: maybe it was just the fact that she had rarely been presented with the opportunity of making a real choice since landing at the hostel? What were the alternatives? More waiting in yet more cafes? Not even the chance to wipe down a table top to make her feel as if she was still part of a world she could understand and care about? The money could buy her a home, documents, new clothes. She knew the score, everyone knew the score – even the policemen who had misinterpreted her honesty. Opportunities didn't come to those who waited. Another lie she could nail – simply by nodding her head to Darko's offer. Nadja finished her espresso and pulled on her jacket ready to leave. She wasn't hungry any more. The breakfast could wait. She couldn't.

'I will do it, Darko.'

'Good. We shall speak again soon.'

Darko stood to let her pass and Nadja left the cafe. She walked at random for hours, flitting up and down streets she had already paced a thousand times, penniless and alone. She kept her head down and concentrated on thinking through what had happened in the cafe. In truth, she had given in. She had become another trader, just like the men on the stairwells who arranged for people to sell their wedding rings, their bodies – even their blood. A woman paid to watch, but never to speak. She remembered the young man who rescued burning words, and tears stung her eyes. Memories weighed heavier than the rain which crashed down on top of her.

'It is a downpour,' she recited to herself. Really, so many new words and just to talk about the weather! More words than she could ever remember. She really had lied to the young man. She wouldn't remember, after all. She would be paid to forget what she had seen, particularly when questioned by anyone. She would become a mute, a shadow. What had really changed in the cafe? Sure, she would have a place to live where the door would finally shut tight and the toilet would flush, but she would still be nothing more than a smudge on the landscape. A camouflage woman. Living below the fold, existing on the edge, stepping into shadow. A lost negative. She was surprised at how many phrases made sense to her now she was to become invisible.

Nadja sat down at the bus stop opposite the hostel. She blew on her fingers to warm them and tapped her toes on the pavement. Three buses slipped past, but she barely registered them. If she walked back into the hostel, she was lost; if she jumped on a bus, she would be lost. She had no destination. It was not a tragedy, just a fact, like blowing up a library, or burying a dead baby. Tragedies happened to people who were famous. They were written up in big headlines and punctuated with photographs. In a climate where the weather had dozens of names to describe it, her kind of story remained wordless.

Nadja stood up and glanced around her. The rain pounded the shelter's glass, which rocked frantically inside its metal frame. She saw him at once, even though he stood in the middle of the rush-hour throng. Zoran waited until he saw that she had recognised him then, almost imperceptibly, he tilted his head towards the street cutting away behind her. Nadja turned round and began walking. He would follow, she knew it. She kept a quick pace and didn't look round again. This is how it would be from now on: a nod, a touch, a whispered word; encounters so fleeting, they would run into each other like the raindrops in a downpour. Nadja stopped. She sniffed the late evening air. She could smell paper burning. She turned round – Zoran was standing behind her. He held a cigarette lighter to a wad of paper. She was close enough to see the writing on the top – it looked like her application for asylum.

'Insurance, Nadja. You know how it is.'

The papers crumbled. Zoran kicked over the dying embers.

'Be here tomorrow evening at nine o'clock, okay? Welcome on board.'

He turned on his heel and was off, before Nadja could reply. She bent down and ran her fingers over the pile of ashes. She hadn't lied, after all. She would remember everything that happened, of course she would, but hadn't she always known she would be silenced, one way or another?

HAND OVER FIST

'It's the hands that do it for me every time,' Maloney said.

'Odd that,' Frankie replied.

Maloney's fascination for hands was well known – further comment from Frankie wasn't necessary. Maloney shifted on top of his bar stool. It was a humid evening in early July. The doors and windows of The Albany were flung wide open. A hum of passing traffic and the whiff of diesel did little to expel the sense that they might as well be sitting inside a sweaty gym shoe. Maloney rubbed his hands over his face. His fingers were long and thin, decorated with silver rings he made up to his own designs. The rings were supposed to detract from the scars. Maloney rebuilt walls. He tore bricks apart, like they were lumps of bread – that's what Frankie said and nobody argued with Frankie, even though he was a birdlike man. His skin was mapped over with thick, blue veins that stood out like discarded spaghetti on his tea-coloured skin. He was broad-shouldered, but his jeans hung loose on his pointy, little arse. Frankie was a *wee dab*, but he could fight cruel.

'You don't have to tell me, Frankie. I *knows* what she's like, all said and done.'

'Dump her then.'

Frankie was known as The Binman, because of the number of women he had dumped over the years. He couldn't stomach his friend's generosity towards women.

'You says what you needs to say, then chips and kips. After all, you's got a bastard brilliant excuse this time round, haven't you? You just got to ring Ollie.'

A week back, Maloney had received an out-of-the-blue telephone call from Ollie Osborne, an old contact from the sites. He wanted to know if they were interested in doing some casual work in the Balkans of all places: there was a Jewish cemetery in Split to be done up, apparently, one of many sites left untended after a recent civil war. Frankie was up for it – cash in hand and Ollie swore Croatia was on the mend and just like the Riviera – but Maloney had stumbled off course again.

'Nell's a special kind of model, see, Frankie.'

'What she model then? Handcuffs?'

'No, hand cream. You know, I'd like to take her fingerprints, like them forensic boys do on the telly.'

'Well, I can understand that, Maloney. Criminal what she done to you. I mean, she stripped you dry as a bone – even took the kettle. Times like these, I despairs of you, man, I really do. You got to make a clean start – take up Ollie's offer. You could even buy yourself a new sun hat.'

Maloney ordered beers and whisky chasers and they carried on drinking in companionable silence. Maloney took in Frankie's hands when he put his glass down. On his left hand he wore an ornate, calligraphic script that spelt out the legend *The Bloobirds*. Thanks to a tattooist who knew how to shape individual letters into something of rare beauty. Frankie's tattoos were choice. Everybody knew about Frankie the Binman's style.

'I wants to try and win her back, I suppose.'

'What's with the suppose, Maloney? Either you do, or you don't – and I think you don't.'

'How do you make that out? My perfect woman, isn't she?'

'She's a bastard one-trick pony, that's all.'

Maloney sighed. Frankie didn't have the whole picture. How could he possibly describe the friction Nell caused inside him? She really understood the power of touch. Truth told, her hands were her only glory – she had a face like a distressed horse and she wore a man's brogues, size twelve. Come to think of it, Frankie could probably sleep in her shoes.

'She's written to me. Says she's sorry, like.'

'For Christ's sake, Maloney. *Ring Ollie.*'

'Okay, okay. I'm shifting.'

Maloney walked home to make the telephone call. The heat in and outside the pub had left him feeling sticky as a lolly. Albany Road was a dirty scab of a place that evening, full of upended bin bags, takeaway wrappers and what appeared to be a student's course notes, scattered in bundles over the paving stones. He bent down and sifted through the handwritten pages lying at his feet, all showing symbols he failed to recognise. A scientist in the making, or a doodle bug with no inclination to study? Maloney couldn't decide which. He gathered up as many sheets as he could hold and dumped them inside one of the split-open bin bags. Days like this, he wished he lived in a tidy, white ribbon of a street, lined with mansions and lilac trees. There might be tidy streets in Croatia, who knew?

Arriving back home, Maloney failed to raise Ollie on his land line, so he sent him a text message instead detailing their proposed arrival time at Split airport. Frankie was right, he thought, retiring to his camp bed – he had got itchy feet. Not much had really happened to him in a long time, even allowing for the odd appearance from a very odd hand-cream model. He had been walled up in a chrysalis of a bedsit, decorated with orange and brown sunflowers. His wings had been clipped, but not for much longer – Ollie would see him right. Maloney made himself a new ring by way of celebration, decorating it with an etching of a map of Split. He found one in an atlas in the city library when he headed off to collect his flight tickets. He placed the map inside a little shield at the front of the ring, a talisman of better things to come. He had been given a free hand in his new contact, after all.

'You got to grab it while you can,' Frankie said, as they boarded the aeroplane to Split.

Walking out of the airport concourse, they barely had time to adjust to the excruciating heat of late July, before Ollie yanked them off to visit the cemetery. They were joined on their trip by Igor, a local builder, and by an interpreter called Anastasia, who gave Maloney no surname, just her miraculously small hand. She was balanced on top of the most extraordinary platform sandals he had ever seen, tied to her skinny legs by what appeared to be yards of leather thong. Maloney concentrated hard. Ollie barked directions at him; Frankie leered because he had clocked him clocking the interpreter; Igor grunted and Anastasia swept the air with her propellor-like hands, gilded with a sparkling blue nail polish. Maloney knew if he watched her hands, he was a dead man. He watched Anastasia's hands. They spoke louder than she did to a man with his tastes. Her fingernails glittered and sweat trickled from her palms down her absurdly tiny wrists. She was built on the same scale as Frankie and projected a similar air of contained violence.

'History is like an elderly person, is it not, Mr Maloney? It needs a regular wash and brush-up, but the politicians they say to me: there is no money.'

Anastasia didn't give him a second's breath to answer. She switched between Croatian and English effortlessly, wending her way in and out of complex grammatical constructions like a limbo dancer. Maloney wasn't so much impressed as blown away by this sprite with her blue fingernails. He stooped towards the sun-cooked paving stones, like a stalking cat. His shoulders bunched forwards in his linen jacket, making a big, cool shadow for the ants that darted over the road's surface. It was close to midday, but already the sun scorched his skin. The cemetery was situated at the top of a hill, behind a cafe popular with tourists who came up to admire the view of the city from its open-air terrace. Maloney paused there himself to take a look at the sea, which circled Split's harbour like a big, blue hand. Stone houses with red-tiled roofs folded themselves into the hills below them.

'The cemetery is just here, Mr Maloney,' Anastasia said, her hand coming to rest on his arm.

Maloney let himself be steered towards the cemetery's iron gates. They stood in a slipshod manner, balanced against each other with the help of a heavy chain. Peering through, he could see the cemetery had shared their fate. The graves nearest to him were little more than piles of loose stones, hidden in an overgrown tangle of grass. Their outlines were just about visible underneath a coat of fallen pine needles. A few boasted chipped carvings of roses, or scrolls inscribed in what he assumed to be Hebrew; a few carried the Star of David. A radio played loudly somewhere inside the cafe, but there was no sign of anybody on the premises. Igor indicated their route into the cemetery by pointing to a small grass bank, which shielded the sight of the tombstones from the cafe terrace. Maloney started to scramble up behind Igor, but then he remembered Anastasia and her impractical platform shoes.

He turned round. Anastasia was kneeling on the ground, slowly unlacing the sandal she had placed in front of her. Her skirt had blown back over her knees and he could see her knickers. Her sandals unlaced, she looked up and fixed Maloney with a stare – she knew he had seen what she wanted him to see. She threw the sandals to him and then scampered up the bank. Maloney tied the sandals round his neck and they walked towards the first of the graves in an uneasy silence. Pine cones crunched under their feet, cicadas chattered noisily in the air and a couple of butterflies danced by Maloney's shoulder. He cut across a row of graves and punched into the butterflies' airborne gavotte, sending them scattering. Maloney walked on. The majority of the graves were open to the skies, their headstones swivelled sideways, like loose shutters. They were all empty. Sweat stung his eyes. Anastasia caught up with him.

'Over here, Mr Maloney, if you please.'

If he pleased! Anastasia gripped his arm and led him further up the hillside cemetery. A less badly damaged grave came into view, its decoration of palm leaf and roses still visible. A wild kitten lay curled up on its base, asleep in the hot sunshine. Maloney knelt down to inspect the inscription:

'Tilde Eschenasi
Da Crudel Morro Rapita
All Affetto
Dei Suoi Cari . . .

'She was my grandmother, Mr Maloney.'

The kitten had woken and fled at the sound of their voices, its spindly legs all wobbly. Maloney had an idea this was how Anastasia would leave his bed, shaky without the sandals to anchor her. He instinctively reached out and found her leg close to his shoulder. He gripped her calf hard. She caught her breath.

'What you saying exactly, Anastasia?'

'My family are buried here. No, my tense is incorrect – they were buried here.'

'You putting up the money for the restoration job, is that it?' Maloney hazarded a guess and landed a bullseye.

'Yes.'

'Seems a lost cause, if you don't mind me saying so. I mean, look at this place. It's on its last legs.'

This reminded him he was still gripping Anastasia's calf. Maloney relaxed his grip. She folded up beside him.

'I can't have justice, but I will have a grave I can visit.'

'It don't make sense to me, that's all.'

He stroked her dusty instep which had edged towards his knee. The others were further back down the hill, caught up in a complicated conversation delivered by hand signals. *Carpe diem*. Would she maybe go for a drink with him? Maloney was about to ask outright, but Anastasia cut in first:

'My grandpa killed Tilde. She didn't want to be killed by the occupiers, so she ask Grandpa to strangle her. Believe me, it happened. And you are thinking: why go back and remember those who are long dead when there are so many new dead to mourn? It is simple, Mr Maloney: it makes the present seem not so terrible.'

Maloney felt himself moving like a blind fish through tangled weed in the face of such a revelation.

'You can tell me more over a drink, Anastasia? Just the two of us, like . . .'

Anastasia shifted on to the back of her heels and stared at him long and hard. A transaction in a graveyard. He had done worse and so had she. He read guilt in her eyes and in her hunched shoulders. A pale smudge at the top of her camisole top revealed where the sun never shone. He suspected her heart had been bleached the same colour over the years from too little heat, too little warmth, just this determination to keep something alive that had been dead and inadequately mourned and buried for half a century, or more. Maloney almost wept. Anastasia shifted on to her knees and took a look over her shoulder to see what the others were up to. Satisfied they were still preoccupied, she turned back to Maloney and offered to show him her family home on the nearby island of Hvar. The house had been lost and then recovered. Anastasia had earnt the money to buy back the house working as an interpreter for the United Nations. Now, she was determined to restore the cemetery. She insisted he take up the work. She would make sure he stayed, Maloney thought, whatever it might take.

He accepted her offer and then walked back down the hill to let the others know of his plans. Frankie whistled, Ollie butted him in the ribs. Ignoring their antics, Anastasia took Maloney's arm again and led him back to the harbour-side. A holiday ferry had taken them to the island. A man carrying a cardboard tray of eggs struck up a conversation with Anastasia. He offered them some of his eggs and they hungrily poured the raw yolks down their dehydrated throats. Disembarking, they climbed up another hill, this one topped with an old Venetian fort that had been turned into a disco for summer tourists. Shortly before reaching the fort, they veered off into a cramped courtyard and Maloney found himself walking beneath a Corinthian-style balustrade, trimmed with vines. A plate of lemons had been left to cool in their shade. The balustrade was part of Anastasia's house, a tall, narrow, stone building with a red-tiled roof. Seen in close-up, the tiles looked like fat sausages.

'They blow off all the time, Maloney. Leaks sprout everywhere.'

Anastasia had dropped the 'Mr' since they set sail. Inside her house, it was surprisingly cold. Maloney shivered and Anastasia rubbed the goose bumps on his bare forearms. The place reeked of the lavender that was harvested on the island. Anastasia showed Maloney into a back room where a quilt had been laid out on the floor. There was mould growing on the wall, evidence of the leaking roof. Maloney applied himself to the job in hand. His brick-raw hands rested like cattle brands on Anastasia's prominent ribcage. She lay still for him, as if acting on an unspoken order. Her eyes closed, but not in abandon. Every trackway of his hands was noted. Maloney felt it was not him as such, but something else beyond his touch. The memory of it seemed to haunt her, as he worked to climax. He turned her on her side and folded her into him. He cupped her breasts in his hands and waited. He expected tears for some reason he couldn't fathom, but was surprised when Anastasia laughed instead. She traced the ring on his finger.

'It's a map, is it, Maloney?'

'Recognise it, do you?'

She pulled the ring up to her eyes.

'It's a map of Split.'

'Thought I might get lost, see.'

'You were wrong.'

'Yes, I was wrong.

They settled back down on the quilt. A breeze distracted him, then the sound of a motorbike revving up in the cobbled streets that lay beyond the open door. Maloney wrapped his hands around Anastasia's. The whole world in his hands. Could it ever be enough? He remembered belatedly Frankie's warning: *hands don't never tell the whole story, Maloney boy*. His mouth was full of Anastasia's hair, but he didn't brush it away. The etched shield on the ring caught the light. He circled it over Anastasia, who had fallen fast asleep crooked inside his elbow. A distant clock struck the hour.

He smelt lavender and lemons on the air. Whichever way he looked at this deal, Maloney couldn't help but feel he had won hands down.

DOG DAYS

Efa counted Jack's fingers splayed on the table. He only had eight. The little fingers were missing. She watched his hands moving amongst the cups and wondered over the significance of the missing fingers. Would her mother ask Jack about them? No, she hadn't. They sat in a cafe in High Street, wedged between half-a-dozen families and couples smoking and bickering. Maybe you couldn't talk about missing fingers when you sat so close to strangers?

'It's supposed to be an Indian summer, Shani, but you gets boiled up like a kipper one minute, and soaked the next.'

Efa's mother laughed. She wore a red suede beret and red lipstick and people were staring at her out of the corner of their eyes. Her Mam was always being watched by somebody, usually a man. Her hair reached down to her hips. When Efa was really tired and it rained and there was nothing else to do, she often folded herself up in the wing of Mam's hair.

'Twinge of the arthritis in the hands,' Jack continued. 'But what about you? Are you all right, after you know, everything?'

49

It was a rainy day in an Indian summer. Rain crashed against the plate-glass windows and Shani pulled her denim jacket tightly around her.

'Freezing in here, isn't it? No, Jack. I'm all right. Can't complain. Well, I could, but who would hear me?'

'I would!'

Efa reminded her mother of her presence, a habit she had got into after Da left home with another woman that wasn't Mam. Their dogs had been killed and the police had taken Mam away in a car. Efa had to go a stranger's home.

'It's all right. Only for a night, lovely,' the police-woman said. 'Very grown up and everything. Imagine, it's like going to a hotel. Have you ever done that before?'

Efa shook her head. She had slept in the caravan all her eight years, alongside her Mam. She didn't even know what a hotel was, but felt shy of asking. The policewoman gave her a KitKat, which she ate lying in a strange bed waiting for her Mam to come and collect her. Efa waited for fourteen hours. What had gone on in all that time? Her Mam was silent when they returned to the caravan.

'Ask no questions, don't get told no lies.'

Her Mam was always saying things like this. Odd bits of advice that Efa found hard to adapt in her world. She asked her Mam things, because she was grown up and she had lived overseas. That was before Efa was born, but she still occasionally dropped in to a different way of talking. She used funny words, which were attractive because of their unusual sound. '*Je t'aime*,' she said, wrapping her in her hair. Efa thought she said 'tame.' She curled up beside her mother and stayed very still. She tried to behave like the greyhounds had when they were after something. Motionless, but observant, waiting for a let-up in the rain, or a titbit from the dinner Mam was cooking.

Jack rolled a cigarette up between his eight fingers. He lent money to the caravan people, bundles of notes tied up with shoe laces. Mam told Efa that Jack 'drove a hard bargain.' Efa knew this meant they would have to give him something in return for the money they were asking to buy new dogs. What had they left to sell? The microwave had gone; the telly had gone; even her school shoes. Mam opened up the breast pocket of her jacket and pulled out a tissue-wrapped parcel. Inside, a pair of earrings that glittered in the strip light shining above their heads. Jack rolled the earrings between his eight fingers. He bit the clasp on each one.

'Gold. Quite a treasure, Shani. Who gave you these then? Never Petey, that's for sure.'

Jack laughed but Mam stayed silent. Efa looked up at her. Her eyes narrowed and her red mouth looked like the unhealed scar on her knee. Petey was Efa's Da, but he had run away two years ago, so of course he couldn't go buying her Mam jewellery!

'Point is: will they get me enough to replace the

dogs, Jack? There's a race this time next week and I mean to be at it. They won't scare me away.'

'The world is tightening its belt and the little man, such as myself, is squashed in the process. No luxury with the belt at top notch.'

'Please, Jack. I need to show at this race.'

Efa looked at her Mam. Tears were crowding her eyes. She slipped her hand in her Mam's and gave it a squeeze.

'They killed our dogs, the bastards. Couldn't stomach success, could they? We'll still race though. I promise us that in my dreams, Efa.'

Jack shook his head. The earrings clicked together in his balled fist.

'Here's what I'll do. I know someone who wants to break into the market, so to speak. You can be a front for him. You race his dogs and keep a share of the profits, *if* you win.'

He dropped the earrings back into Shani's waiting palm. She bit her lip and drew blood. Efa put up her finger and wiped her Mam's lips clean.

'I've no choices left, have I?'

Jack sighed. Efa understood that he didn't want to make her mother cry anymore, but for some reason she didn't understand that nobody wanted to buy earrings, just tighten their belts. Outside in High Street, rain thundered down and the gutters flooded. A bus hurtled past them and a wave of puddle water drenched their legs.

'Bastard!' Shani yelled.

She ran out into the gutter and jumped up and down in her anger. Efa joined her Mam. They jumped up and down together and they were like raindrops themselves, falling on the world and bouncing back up as high as the sky. Back home in the caravan, it was terribly cold. Their bar fire had broken, so they went to bed early. Mam put night lights around the bunk bed where they slept. Her face was snowdrop pale in the half-light. She unearthed extra blankets from a wooden chest and piled them up on top of their bed. They nestled in wool and Efa tried to forget about Jack's missing fingers – and the missing money.

'Won't we have greyhounds no more, Mam?'

'I don't know, Efa. Not for the foreseeable future.'

'Is it because Da's not here that we don't have no money to buy new dogs?'

'Sort of. It was always a pinch, even with him here. Don't you remember?'

Efa tried to think back to the past, but she couldn't get past the scene in the cafe where her mother had cried, because the earrings that Petey hadn't bought her were not going to make them any money.

'I remember Da best. Are his shoes full of worms, Mam?'

'Ssh. Ssh. Why do you ask such questions?'

'I dream about him too, Mam. He has slime in his eyes. His glasses are made out of eyes. His lips are slime too.'

53

Mam pulled her under her wing of hair and held her so tight she thought she might stop breathing.

'Please God, no more talk, like this!'

'Have I frightened you?'

'You've frightened me stupid.'

'It's the dream I have, Mam.'

'He's keeping his head low somewhere, that's what it is, Efa. But we don't need him, do we? There's you and me. And there's Jack and his plan.'

Efa was too tired to question Mam further. She slept in late the next morning. Woke after midday, sun dappled on the rugs around her. Mam had kohl-coloured sleepy dust in her eyes. Efa picked it out with her finger tip.

'So whose dogs will we race now?'

Ever since she could remember, Mam had raced greyhounds. It was her passion. She trained her dogs and she knew how to nurse them. That's how she met Da. His champion racer had taken a fall in a rabbit hole. She made a splint out of kindling wood and old sheets and placed special herbs between the twists of cloth. The dog won in his first race after recovery. Da had taken her with him to the track and she bet £10 and won nearly £400. They were quite a partnership, she told Efa. But now she was to race a stranger's dogs. The stranger had introduced himself a few days after the meeting in the cafe. Jack was as good as his word.

'A rare quality in a man,' said Mam.

Mr Cole was very tall. He stooped to stand in the

caravan. He was dressed in a baseball hat and a navy blue fleece. He barely looked at Shani all the while they talked.

'I've been banned from the racing, see. There was allegations made about me doping my dogs, but it was just a trace of chemicals from the chocolate drops I fed them. They wanted me to pay a fortune to get a second opinion, but where would I get the money, I says to them? I need another route in. Jack tells me you're clean. You can race, but you don't have no dogs.'

'My dogs were killed, Mr Cole.'

'I heard something about that. I'm sorry. They were both winners too.'

'So was my man. Once upon a time.'

Efa saw them exchange a look. It was as if her Mam were signalling something to this Mr Cole. She was down and out, but not beaten. She wouldn't take any lip, not like some of the other site women did when they were left on their own. Efa wedged herself between her Mam and Mr Cole, just to be on the safe side. Mr Cole patted her head, as if she were one of his dogs. She could hear them whining outside the caravan.

'Show us the dogs, Mr Cole. Go on.'

Mr Cole smiled. He was missing his two front teeth. In their place, two gold tombstones. Efa asked him to bend down, so she could tap them with her fingers.

'Where'd they go?'

'To heaven.'

'What? Two teeth on their own?'

'Why not? Alone doesn't mean you can't share in the best things in life, if you so choose.'

Efa hadn't understood his odd answer, but she suspected it might be directed at Mam. She was looking more like her usual self. She wore a vest top and Levi's. The tops of her breasts showed above the lace trim on her vest. They had freckled up like a bird's eggs.

'Go and look at the dogs, Efa. Quick now.'

Mr Cole pulled two string leads out of his jeans back pocket.

'You want to walk them?'

Efa raced out of the caravan and discovered the dogs sitting at the bottom step, whining and whimpering for a show of their owner. She fussed them and got their leads on. Mr Cole shouted out encouragement from behind the door. She heard murmuring. There was to be more chat with her Mam, but she was to walk the dogs. Efa had to lift them over the stile that separated the site from the fields beyond. She let them off the leads once they reached the back field, which circled the caravan site like a big, straggly eyebrow. She found a lid discarded from a paint pot and used it as a frisbee to keep the dogs running back to her. The dogs were called Jet and Chalky. Spindly legs and ribs that stuck out in corrugated waves under their skin, but when they moved, they were like water. Liquid fast. Efa roamed with the dogs for over an hour. Breathless and hungry, she rounded them up and got them back to the caravan. Mam sat on the steps with Mr Cole. He had his shirt off and he was a skinny rib too. His arms were covered with strange geometric shapes, which Efa traced with her fingers.

'Da only had the one tattoo, Mr Cole. He had a serpent on his shoulder blade. Just there.'

She pushed her fingers into his back, just above the right shoulder blade. He winced.

'Don't pester, Efa,' warned her Mam.

They were going to race Mr Cole's dogs and they were going to pretend that they were theirs and split the winnings. A simple plan. Mr Cole had raced in the North East, but never in Wales so no one would recognise his dogs. Her Mam filled her in with all the details, as she washed Efa in the zinc basin they used for a bath. Efa noticed bruising on her Mam's neck, just below her ear. She knew it was something to do with Mr Cole, but it was not a bad thing. Mam was smiling. Efa liked it when her Mam smiled. She hadn't done much smiling since Da had gone away.

One week later, they were standing together watching Jet and Chalky hit the track at the racecourse that lay behind High Street. A blur of legs and muzzles. Jet was No 9 and Chalky was No 13. Unlucky 13, Efa thought with alarm as they put the racing number on her shivering back. Chalky's muzzle sniffed the air and found victory. Jet had come third. Chalky had gone so fast, Efa had hardly been aware of her legs moving at all. Mam stood smoking roll-ups. Her freckled breasts poked through her mohair jumper which had slipped away from her shoulders. The men around her whispered and stared. Mam collected her winnings, her snakeskin boots glinting in the stadium's spotlights.

No one clapped or congratulated her, but so what? Hadn't Mam always defied those who claimed Da was a cheat and sold sick dogs? They had never wanted her parents on the track, simple as. So, their dogs were poisoned and their neighbours on site whispered Mam had committed a murder. The police hunted for what they thought might be a missing body. How could they think a whole body had gone missing? Efa often wondered. Two fingers, sure, but her Da's body with its serpent tattoo coiling around his shoulder blade?

Mr Cole met them two days later in the cafe in High Street. Mam had wrapped his share of the bank notes up in a newspaper. He tucked it into his leather jacket, like a baby in a papoose.

'How's tricks?'

He ruffled Efa's hair and gazed all the while at her Mam. Efa knew his secret, before he even had a chance to deny it. He was in love with her Mam. He watched her stub out a roll-up in the ashtray. She had tobacco on her teeth, a bruise on her neck, but she was as powerful as a dog pitched to race. She returned Mr Cole's gaze. Efa was shy of them both as they sat silently watching each other.

'Will we race Jet and Chalky again, Mr Cole?'

'Dermot. The name's Dermot.'

'Will we race the dogs again, please, Dermot.'

'I think we probably will, little lady.'

Efa recalled the scene at the race track, as they walked up to the crash barrier with the binoculars to pick out Chalky and Jet. A terrible thought came over her as she gazed at Mr Cole's golden teeth.

'You won't disappear too, Mr Cole . . . Dermot?'

Mam's mouth made the scar shape again. Efa wondered if she could run as fast as Chalky to get away from the terrible look she gave her. Mr Cole ruffled her hair again.

'I'm a careful man, Efa. I put my money where my gob is and keep it tight shut. It'll do me.'

Efa looked over at her mother.

'Dermot is right, lovely. We can't ever know for sure what *might* happen, particularly when things go bellyside up.'

Mr Cole brushed Mam's cheekbone with the back of his hand.

'Da moved on, see, and left me to deal with everything. I didn't know how to explain it all properly, you being so young an' all. And you were missing the dogs too, weren't you?'

Mr Cole put an arm around Efa's shoulders.

'I'm going to race Chalky again under your Mam's name. Will we have another win, do you think?'

Mam smiled encouragement. Efa remembered how defiant and victorious she had looked on the race track. It was a safe bet she would never go walkabout, unlike Da.

'If we win, can we buy back the telly, Mam?'

'We can do better than that,' Mr Cole interjected. 'We shall buy ourselves a cinema and a popcorn machine!'

Efa thought this a sensible investment, what with the Indian summer being full of rain and the caravan springing leaks. They could sit in their cinema and wait out the downpour. Efa smiled at her Mam and at Dermot. She missed many things, for sure, just like Jack must do his fingers, but there were surprises that made up for the absences. Surprises were a kind of secret, after all. They were secrets unravelled and shared, unlike the one that surrounded her Da's whereabouts. Efa left the table and went to pet Chalky and Jet, who had been left outside the cafe. She fed them pieces of her iced sponge cake. Granules of sugar stuck fast to their wet muzzles.

'We're winners all over again,' she whispered. 'Da, or no Da.'

SALT & BLOOD

When the drought began, the council put a water tap on site but it was empty when Caitlin tried turning it on.

'What we wash in then?' she asked Howell. 'Dust baths?'

Howell emptied handfuls of earth over her pale yellow hair. Later, they stole water from buckets left in garages by keen suburban gardeners, crawling in through the tiniest of gaps and discovering the basins stored in the dark. They filled old petrol cans and plastic water bottles and took them home, balanced on their heads. That's how it was done in faraway countries, Howell said. Truth was, he was only showing off to Nia. She sometimes tagged along, but she never stole water supplies for her Mam. She just chewed gum and tried to make her school skirt look shorter by folding up her waistband. Her legs were cottonwool soft, covered with insect bite scabs – everybody on the site had unsightly rashes and dry patches of skin that summer.

'You need to drink more water,' said the health visitor.

But the tap hadn't come on and there was no rain for

what seemed like months so the river bed had cracked up like an old dinner plate. The earth baked hard and frogs and fish choked in the dust.

'Who would expect to have sun in summer,' joked Caitlin's Da.

'Not even picking with rain now, is it?'

Each morning, they checked the clump of seaweed hanging outside the caravan door, but it remained bone-leather dry. Caitlin thought her brain had turned into the same horrible texture. In school, she flicked dead flies on to her classmates' necks. When she was told to stop, she pushed her desk over and ran away – down to the river bank where the grass beneath her crackled under her weight. She stayed away from school for days on end, falling asleep on the burnt-out grass. Waking up, Caitlin was convinced her skin would crack open if she so much as smiled. Mam rubbed some of her precious Nivea cream into her skin each night, but it was still sun-sore the next day.

'Sleep tight, little fright.'

Her Da sitting at the foot of her bed, his shoulders slumped forwards into his too-large shirt. He was small and thin and his clothes never seemed to fit properly, but he was greedy as a crow. He rode the horses and he sold the horses they kept tethered in the field beyond the flyover. Howell helped him out. Howell was fifteen. He tasted of salt. Caitlin carried his baby.

'You could have swallowed a pickle whole!' said Da.

Another of his jokes, but Caitlin's body ached in an

odd way and the hot, dry nights kept her awake and restless. Da sat with her and talked to her about the horses. Caitlin didn't like being alone with her growing belly. Mam said not to worry, but it was different for her. She had borne five children and had got used to her body growing away from her – folding her curves into the mouths and hands of her husband and children. Sometimes, at the horse fairs, she drank a little too much and she danced, but Caitlin couldn't help feeling her Mam's body looked all wrong without another wrapped around it. Mam danced slowly, as if afraid her wide hips might knock over a ghost child that floated around her. There were four ghosts Caitlin knew about – four babies who had never made the journey out into a world of dust and frogs.

In the early evening, Da fed the horses then sat with Caitlin on the caravan steps. He promised that when the river was full again, they would teach her baby to swim. He made plans, but they were always far ahead in the distance. Caitlin wondered how they would fill all the in-between time, particularly as the heat made everything so slow. Everybody on the site trod their lives in lead shoes the summer the drought came. The health visitor warned Caitlin that the police might get involved with the birth of her baby. Caitlin imagined a constable delivering her baby into his upturned hat and laughed. She was fourteen, the health visitor pointed out. Technically, she was in breach of the law and so was Howell, but still they lay together by the river.

Making love in its carpet of dust, they unearthed the mummified remains of dead frogs and fishes. The hospital scan showed Caitlin's baby to be a frog-baby floating deep inside her, deep down under her belly button.

'If I gets hotter, will the baby dry up?'

The health visitor reassured her. She urged Caitlin to drink more milk. She would chase up the council about the water tap. Howell went back to the sprinkler-fed gardens and picked up windfalls. Apples, plums and pears. Their fruit-sticky skin excited them and Caitlin made love to Howell once more, his hands resting on top of her swollen stomach. She was worried they might make another baby and there wouldn't be room inside her for double the number of heads and limbs. Caitlin felt her balance shift and sway. The endless foraging for water had exhausted her. She began to believe Howell hated her new, big belly. He preferred to walk out with Nia, whilst Caitlin stayed at home.

'Sleep tight, little fright,' she whispered down to her stomach.

As she drifted into sleep, her baby poked its way around her pouch of a belly. The hot nights were no barrier to its kicking legs. She could see the shadow of a foot flexing on her pale stomach. Mam was pleased. She wrapped her hands round Caitlin's belly and cried. Caitlin knew then her life would always be different. She would stay different, even after her baby was born and her stomach was as flat as paper again. She was going to be a mother. She would move like a Mam, slowly and heavily, as if always in anticipation of the hands and mouths that would touch and eat her in the future, hungry like she had been for the stolen plums. It wasn't the same hunger that Howell felt for her. Caitlin cried, but not because she was happy. She felt dead and buried, like one of the river frogs.

Mam rubbed oil in to her stomach. She made endless brews and Caitlin found herself constantly going to the toilet. The toilet was a plastic bucket. She emptied it out on the baked ground and watched the soil fizz and froth. Howell left her some more windfall apples – they had been chewed up by wasps and were as brown as the dusty earth she trod in. This time, Caitlin felt his offering was made out of guilt, rather than from choice. He avoided the caravan, so Mam had taken her shopping up town when the next Giro came through. Mam looked at the slope of Caitlin's belly and pronounced she had a granddaughter on the way. They bought baby grows in shades of 'apple blossom pink.' Caitlin looked at the colour photographs on the shop walls displaying beautiful toddlers in a variety of seasonal outfits. The grass they tumbled on was green; the flowers framing their heads a riot of red and yellow. Caitlin thought the colours must have been painted on to the photograph, they were so bright.

That night, she dreamt about her frog-baby swimming in red and yellow water. Caitlin woke up, her body soaked with sweat. She changed the sheets and then she sucked on an ice cube to keep her temperature down – she still wasn't convinced that she couldn't cook her own baby, if she got too hot. The next morning, Howell unexpectedly called round. Nia was in tow, her hair braided so tight on her head it had pulled her eyes upwards into the shape of two cuticle moons. Caitlin wrenched up the rug hanging over the window and watched them loiter by the caravan's steps. They didn't touch, but she sensed they probably had some time recently – down on the dusty river bed, or maybe in a semi-lit garage on a water-hunting trip.

Howell rolled a cigarette between dusty fingers. Caitlin watched Nia watching Howell lick up his cigarette papers. He let her light the cigarette, but she fumbled with the matches. He joshed her, his fingers dancing on her bare arms. Caitlin had seen enough. Anxiously, she hurried out of the caravan, but she missed her footing. She tumbled headlong down the caravan's fold-away steps, landing clumsily on her stomach. Howell dropped his cigarette and ran over to catch her, but he was too late. He let her curl up inside his arms and told her to try and sleep.

'Sleep tight, Caitlin. I don't bite, do I?'

Nia picked up the cigarette and brought it over to him.

'Shall I stay too, Howell?'

'I'll catch you laters,' he replied.

Caitlin closed her eyes – she didn't want to see them exchange looks, or anything else come to that. She must have fallen asleep for a long time, because when she woke up, she was alone and the day had cooled down. Flies scudded up and down her skin, like skaters. There was no sign of Howell – bar the small pile of cigarette butts littering the bottom of the caravan steps. A cold band of air brought the hairs up on her neck. The rain when it came fell so hard, the soil sprung up around her. Caitlin felt a hot wave of pain build up inside her. She felt the rain hiss on her skin, but the hot wave inside her wasn't quelled. It rose up and fell, again and again. She sat down on the top step and wrapped her arms around her boiling centre. Mam found her eventually. She tried to unhook her when she saw the blood on the steps, but Caitlin made a vice of her arms and refused to be moved. The blood kept on coming – the rain kept on falling.

In the hospital, her baby was cut out of her. Caitlin swam in hot waves, her throat scorched with pain. They tried to explain how her daughter's heart had grown outside her tiny body – she had breathed in and out and it had killed her. They let her baby lie on her and she snuffled up her smell. Salt and blood. The day passed. Her Mam sat beside her, stroking her hair and the baby's crumpled forehead.

'It happens, Caitlin,' she consoled. 'Sometimes they leave us, before we are ready to let them go.'

Caitlin was reminded of the river frogs, their dried-up skins suffocating them as they waddled in the dusty river bed. Her body was a grave – it was as empty as the summer river. Caitlin lay back on her pillows; she folded herself away from the world and slept.

When she woke up again, her Mam was still sat beside her. She never left Caitlin all the while she stayed in hospital. Mam and her ghostly babies crowding round the narrow hospital bed; Mam busying herself with cups of tea and visitors and bunches of withered flowers. The sun had come out again, after the rain. It was hot to boiling, nothing in-between. Mam dropped ice cubes down Caitlin's nightdress and they giggled, like children might do, at their game.

DAISY, DAISY,
GIVE ME YOUR ANSWER DO

'Will you please listen to me, Ivo?'

A plea, not a question. Ivo stumbled hard against Mack's coffin lid, propped on the wall. Drunk a long time since – no counting the days. Someone had wedged three large asters inside Mack's closed fist.

'Boxer don't want no bastard flowers in his paws, do he, Eric?'

Ivo slipped down the wall, soft as a stocking. Eric reached out, but he was too late. The lid crashed down against the coffin.

'Jeezus and bastard heck!'

Eric lifted up the skewwhiff lid. He blushed as red as the flowers when the funeral parlour receptionist popped her head round the door, the back of her hand clipped to her steel-plate hairdo.

'Can you *please* shut up in here? You should be paying your last respects, not playing the fool.'

'*Don't want to bump no more with no big, fat woman . . .*' Ivo sang back at her.

The woman righted her ruffled blouse over her

admittedly sturdy frame. She cast the evil eye at the drunk man,

'Five minutes you got to get him out of here, Mr Tippett, then I calls the police.'

She slammed the door shut. Ivo keeled over on to his side and threw up down his trouser leg.

'You're a nightmare,' wailed Eric.

'Leastways I'm alive, old pal.'

'Not unless we get you cleaned up, before Ma shows.'

'She's used to me.'

'Selfish bastard. Why don't you call her tune, just for a change?'

'I got me a suit, didn't I?'

'But it's ruined now, Ivo, lad.'

Eric propped the coffin lid back up against the wall and then added the drunk man to the parade. Ivo was pale as breakfast lard, his eyes bloodshot. The small antechamber stank of his vomit and cheap aftershave. Eric scratched his head.

'Laurel and Hardy we is, because this is another fine mess you've got me into.'

Ivo yawned in reply.

'Hot in here, Eric, innit? I's going to take forty winks. Sort the trousers, eh?'

He was asleep, before Eric could argue to the contrary. How strip a man down to his boxers in the middle of a funeral parlour, he puzzled. Mack was going to be no help to him, that much was certain, lying where he was, clutching at his daisies. Eric sat down on the other side of the coffin lid and worked through the options. Number one, get away on his toes, number two . . . he couldn't think of any alternatives. The room was as hot as a racehorse's flank. His shirt stuck to his back. A commotion outside the door of the antechamber alerted him to another possibility: Ma walking in and the trousers becoming a subject of even more heated discussion. As if in reply, the receptionist in the fussy pink blouse poked her head round the door for a second time.

'Someone else to see Mr McGonigle,' she called out.

Eric barely had time to stand upright, before Ma and her entourage swept into the room.

Ma, slim as a pipecleaner, flanked by Ivo's twin younger brothers. Fred and Tolley were the width of the abandoned coffin lid, their huge shoulders ripping at the sleeves of their identical black jackets. They boasted hammerhead fists but were both self-conscious in the suits and the slip-ons that replaced their customary work boots. Ma was dressed in a tiny black coat with an astrakhan collar. The heels of her thigh-high boots were as thin as the stems on a wine glass. Not for the first time Eric wondered over the age of this minuscule woman – gone fifty, but looking younger than Ivo, who was thirty or thereabouts. Ma always hazy on exact ages. She never wanted to pin anything down, unless it were a roll of notes owing her. Ma's blue eyes fixed on his own. She was wearing false eyelashes and a lot of eyeliner.

'Never mind the sulk on your face, Eric. What you gonna do about it?'

Ma could lay down a challenge like John Wayne – truth told, her legs were cowboy bandy in the patent-leather boots.

'Dry cleaners should do the trick, Ma. I'll get them there in a jiffy.'

'You been shoved in preservatives too?'

Tolley sniggered the girly laugh that was so at odds with his thick, veiny neck and too-thin mouth. Fred didn't smile. Fred, in fact, rarely smiled – Ivo said it was because he was shy of his teeth. They were in a dreadful state from the fights he took on. Fred only let girls kiss him on the lips – never tongues. Eric was distracted by his crazy thoughts, because he realised he was at cross-purposes with Ma. She was not one to cross, even without the big boots on her. She stepped over to his side of the coffin and glanced down at the body of her dead husband.

'Who brought them, then?'

'They was here when we arrived, Ma.'

'I said: who brought them?'

'Dunno.'

Ma pushed Eric out of her way and aimed a kick at her son's supine body. He groaned, then belched. He was coming round, slow, slow, slowly, but not fast enough for Ma. She grabbed his head and swung it against the wall, just as the receptionist returned accompanied by the undertaker and two of his assistants. Their funereal demeanour gave way to a clamour of shrieks and nervous giggles.

'Mrs McGonigle!' screamed Miss Dagleish, the receptionist.

'Will you put that man down?' Mr Richards, the undertaker, added for good measure.

Ma dropped her son back on to the floor. He was wide awake now and aware that his situation was probably a lot graver than that of his recently departed father.

'You're getting paid, so don't go interfering none,' warned Ma.

Her heels clicked hard on the parquet floor. Tolley and Fred loomed up over the undertaker. Even his top hat didn't make him a match for the McGonigle brothers. Eric felt responsible somehow. He had let Ivo drink himself into this mess.

'Shall we calm down . . .' he began, but Ma interrupted him.

'What's calm got to do with the price of camels?' she asked.

'You tell me this: who brought them pansy flowers in here?'

'The *aster daisies* came this morning, Mrs McGonigle,' the receptionist replied.

'A man brought them in.'

Eric watched disbelief spread like a rash across Ma's face. Serves her right, he thought. She had assumed the worst and now she had it – in spades.

'A man? What did he look like?'

'Tall, thin build. Dark crew cut. Blue linen shirt, casual cut, like. Oh, and a diamond ring worn on his pinkie.'

The assembled mourners and funeral parlour staff digested the receptionist's description, which she ticked off on her fat fingers with a smug air. A woman who liked to take centre stage, but there were two to tango in the spotlight that particular morning. Ma pulled herself together. She walked up to the coffin and snatched up the daisies.

'He don't go nowhere with those. Not even six feet under.'

She flung them at Ivo.

'You get cleaned up and then you get moving,' she added, before sweeping out of the antechamber, Fred and Tolley in tow.

'It's okay to load the car?' Mr Richards asked.

'Are we off on a bastard holiday then?' Eric replied.

The lid was hammered down on top of Mack by way of reply and his coffin was heaved up onto three pairs of shoulders. The cortege released itself from the room, like a winkle from its shell. Once they had departed, Miss Dagleish returned to the fray, armed with a large can of air freshener.

'We've got Mrs Dougal being laid out at eleven, as you well know,' she announced.

Eric stopped himself from giving her a sarcastic reply. Didn't he have an unusual request he wanted to make of her? He smoothed down his hair, pulled up his coat lapels and followed her back to the reception desk.

'Miss Dagleish. A word, if you please.'

The receptionist's heavily powdered features were lined up against those of a resin-coated Cupid – according to the card propped at its chin, it was the most popular funeral ornament sold by Richards, Gammon & Brake.

'My apologies for our man in there. He doesn't know when to stop, truth be told . . .'

'I can see that for myself, Mr Tippett.'

She was Frosty the Snow Woman, but Eric knew he would have to thaw her if he was to get things straight for Ma.

'Would you know of a dry cleaners round here that can get a pair of trews ship-shape, Bristol fashion, within the hour?'

'Ye Gods and little fishes!' Miss Dagleish raised her eyes heavenwards, in parallel with those of the Cupid beside her.

'Try *Clean As A Whistle* on High Street. You'll have to pay extra, mind.'

'Money no object, Missus.'

'Miss!'

'Miss.'

'And would you have a spare pair of trousers for his lordship in the meantime?'

'And can you tell me what this says?'

Miss Dagleish tapped her red painted finger nail against her name badge

'Richards, Gammon & Brake: Funeral Services.'

'Anything in there about bespoke tailoring?'

'Well, no, but it was worth a try, don't you think?'

Miss Dagleish cast another frost-laden look in his direction. Eric cast a look at his wristwatch: 10. 45 am.

'You've got another "client" coming in at 11 o'clock, isn't that so?'

'I'll get someone to check for you,' she relented.

'We sometimes have spare clothes left here. Tramps and suchlike. Their things get left unclaimed, is what I mean.'

'Sounds perfect. He's got a 28 inch leg.'

'He's going to like it, or lump it, Mr Tippett.'

Eric sat out front leafing through sample books for engraved headstones, whilst the hunt for the right – or nearly right – pair of trousers was made. Ten minutes later, a pair of rather well-worn pinstripes were delivered to Miss Dagleish.

'Seek and ye shall find,' Eric said.

Returning to the antechamber, he discovered Ivo had adopted a crucifix pose, flat on his back, just where the coffin of his late father had stood.

'Entering into the spirit . . .' he chortled.

'You're sobering up, lad.'

Eric had misgivings about this. Ivo sober was even more problematic than Ivo drunk. He tugged his soiled trousers off and replaced them with the borrowed pair.

They were several sizes too big. He took off his trouser belt and fixed it round Ivo's belly.

'It will have to do, boy. Now, let's be having you. We'll meet back at The Four Feathers, after I gets these to the dry cleaners.'

Ivo was up on his feet, although he still looked dazed.

'What was those bastard flowers about, Tippy? Da ain't no queer sort, was he, now?'

'No, no, lad. Get us to the funeral and we'll hear all. Could be a fan, I suppose. Dozens of the bastards turning out, I hears. They wants to mourn the passing of one of the greatest bare-knuckle boxers there has ever been – sod the likes of Black Jack and his threats.'

Ivo gripped Eric's shoulder – he had a tight hold, even with the punishment he had had from the drink. From now on, he would be called out all hours of the night and day to defend the title he had inherited from his father, the one and only Mack McGonigle.

'Black Jack going to put in an appearance, do you reckon, Eric?'

'He would be lynched, if he did. Cheat and a biter an' all . . .'

'Let's not dwell on his positive qualities, eh, Tippy?'

Ivo smiled a McGonigle smile: teeth bared, vicious as a panther. Eric remembered the first time he had seen Mack smile – he had knocked out a challenger with one blow and he had ended up lying across his feet, like a sacrifice. Mack was King of the Gypsies. He took on any challenger and was a sure-fire winner, until

Black Jack came on the scene – drunk, but scheming. There were no holds barred. He took Mack's head between his fists like he was going to plant a kisser on his lips, but instead pushed it through a wooden stall. His face was cut up into bloodstained confetti. The McGonigles had borne a grudge ever since, big as a bear.

'I says, will you listen to me, Ivo? Don't take on no challenges, even if he shows.'

Ivo was unflinching. He was either the most courageous man in the world, or a lamb going to slaughter in the silliest pair of ballooning trousers Eric had ever seen.

'For your Ma's sake then . . .'

'She'd want me to put up a fight.'

'Not if it meant getting blood on those bastard boots of hers.'

Ivo laughed. They had reached the street and a light rain was falling – what Mack had always called 'a clearing-up shower'.

'She's the glam puss all right, isn't she, Eric?'

'Leopard under the finery, mind.'

'Oh, aye. Eats fellas for breakfast.'

'What I think is this: let her remember her Mack as he was. A fighter of the old school. Let's not mess with these Johnny-come-latelies and their backyard wrestling tricks. Isn't that the way of it, today of all days?'

Ivo turned on his heel – his eyes were damp at the corners. He gripped Eric's hand between his scarred fingers.

'You was his butty, through thick and thin. I knows this, but I also knows what I got to do.'

Eric felt a lump in his throat. He loved the bastard, like he was his own. Hadn't he ridden for the midwife through an electric storm that had disrupted an entire county's fuel supply, but left Ma triumphant? Baby Ivo, nine pounds and two ounces and covered in red fuzz, like a baby fox. Mack skipping with his ropes and shouting out *I'm the main man, sure I am*. Ivo had departed, leaving Eric standing in Memory Lane, his hand stinging from his embrace. Eric rubbed his eyes free of tears, then crossed the road to where *Clean As A Whistle* stood. A scrawny woman stood behind the counter, her nylon shirt making her look bleached as a bone.

'Trousers to go, Miss.'

'One hour, sir?'

'That's the ticket.'

'You not got one of them yet. Till's busted, see? We got to wait for the manager, like.'

'I'll take an IOU from a Princess like yourself.'

'Get away.'

'On honeymoon, is it? And me old enough to be your Grand Daddy-O?'

The shop girl grinned. Her front teeth stood at right angles to each other. There was a silver hoop pierced through her bottom lip. How did you kiss with that on, wondered Eric? Eventually, the manager arrived and wrote out a receipt for the trousers. Eric made his way to the pub where Ivo was busy downing shorts and pints, as if his supply might end on the morrow.

'A whisky in the jar, landlord, for Mack McGonigle's right-hand man.'

A cluster of mourners gave way to him. They knew his status, all right. Eric knocked back his drink and held out his glass. Ivo threw a daisy head into it.

'They was from Black Jack all along.'

'Ah, ha,' Eric replied.

'Wants to fight me up on the racecourse. Give us both a sendoff that way, he says.'

The crowd of onlookers bayed their disapproval at the outright contempt shown to their man – bets were already being laid on the fringes of the scene. Eric picked the daisy out from his glass.

'What you gonna do, Ivo, boy?'

At that moment, past and present made a play for each other. Eric remembered holding Mack's bleeding face together, whilst Ma started up the Mini to get him to A&E. The red flower in his hands put him in mind of the event. History repeating itself, he muttered.

'He'll cheat.'

'We're ready for him,' called out one brave heart, dressed in a paisley cravat and a pork pie hat.

'Forearmed is forewarned . . .' said another, his pint shaky in his hand.

'All the same . . .'

'Least said, soonest mended,' Ivo added, slipping his arm round Eric's neck.

'I'm always there for you, lad,' he replied, crushing the daisy inside his fist.

'Don't you think I don't knows that, Eric?'

The coffin lay on a cart in the middle of High Street, draped in black silk. Four horses stood at its head. Their neighing had alerted the drinkers to their stations. A path was made for Ivo and Eric and they had reached the pub door, like visiting royalty, shaking hands as they went – Ivo stepping out stately and assured, just like his father. It could never be a funeral, plain and simple, Eric realised. Besides, things were done differently nowadays. Daisies thrown down by way of challenge into the hands of a dead man. You couldn't libel him maybe, but you could certainly make a pig's bollocks of his lying-in-state. The funeral cortege assembled in neat formation: the black horses pulling the coffin; Ma and her sons straight behind them; two rows of close relatives at their heels and then Mack's fans spilling out over the paving stones like so many bags of sugar. Eric got into place. He had been invited to walk behind Ivo. He was chuffed with the privilege and tried not to spoil it by worrying about the daisies and Black Jack. The cortege was on the verge of departing High Street when a voice called out:

'Your trousers, Mr Tippett!'

The dry cleaning assistant was running across the road, the freshly pressed trousers fluttering above her head. The crowd roared.

'You on a fashion parade, or what, Tippy?'

Ivo restored order to the situation. He negotiated a halt and retreated to the pub's toilet to put his clean trousers on. He reappeared to more cheers and ribaldry, but he put his hand up and stilled the crowd.

'Mack is dead. Long live Mack!'

His supporters yelled and hooted. Ma bit her lips and threaded her tiny arms through Tolley's and Fred's. A commotion broke out at the back of the assembled throng. The crowd made way and revealed another posse of 'mourners': Black Jack and his cohorts armed with planks of wood and iron bars. There wasn't a sound now, aside from the horses' pulling at their bits.

'You is a yellow bastard, Mackie Junior.'

'No one yellow around here,' Ivo parried.

'Yeah? No sign of you earlier. Conclusions get drawn.'

'They can get redrawn.'

Black Jack was as white as an albino, six feet four and thin as string. Ivo appraised the situation – only one chance to get it right.

'You and me. The rest step aside.'

'No, Ivo. We got us Da to bury . . .'

Ma's anguish an upper cut to his side, but a lesson had to be given. Ivo suddenly as quick as a kingfisher. He swooped down on Black Jack, delivering a jab to his chin and then to his belly. He winded him and tripped him up, then sank down on his chest and anchored him to the tarmac. Ivo bit deep into his cheek and spat out skin and gristle.

'Daisy boy,' he shouted out in triumph.

The genuine mourners circled the men holding the iron bars. A few clattered to the ground as hands went up and shoulders were shrugged. Black Jack wheezed like an emptying balloon. Ma walked up to Ivo and kissed him on his bloody lips.

'Now son, are we going to get to this bastard funeral, or no?'

The crowd let its edginess turn into ecstatic approval of Ma and her brood. They filed up behind the coffin, avoiding the recumbent body of Black Jack. The horses pulled on the traces and the cortege was round the corner in a trice. Eric let them go, before walking over to the injured man.

'Here, wear this in remembrance for a true king.'

He dropped the remains of the daisy into Black Jack's open mouth and then shut it up again, tight as a trap.

TOMORROW, IT IS

There wasn't much light left. The fire smoked and the dog was restless. Trees argued with themselves in the cold wind. Dean picked up sticks and ranged them round the fire to dry. His finger nails were thick, like old ivory. He patched them together with superglue to keep their length. Early evening – and there was still time to kill. He tapped out a tempo on his glass of water, improvising within a set pattern of twelve beats. Tap, tap, tap. His dog Walter was curious. He flapped his ears to the rhythm of the drumming nails. Dean laughed and tapped a series of more complex rhythms. The dog's ears flopped down, suddenly useless in the duet he had been conducting with the man. He slid forwards on his haunches; his muzzle nudged his knee.

'We'll go soon.'

Dean rubbed his dog's throat. His eyes closed, seduced by his touch. He knew that look well, but it was all wrong on Walter. He carefully shielded the long nails of his right hand. He didn't want them to break before he had a chance to play again. The fire hissed and he knew he couldn't rescue it. The wood he had gathered was too damp. The ground he sat on was too damp.

Walter shifted from his knee and rounded on the dead fire. He liked heat, did Walter. He sniffed the ground around the flames, moving in as close as he dared. His head darted round when Dean lit a match to his cigarette.

'Here now,' he cajoled.

He turned his palm upwards and the long nails stretched out beyond the fleshy pads of his fingers. Walter stretched out his tongue to lick his skin. Dean was put in mind of a woman he knew who was also obsessed by hands, the many hands that had taken her and then given her back to herself. Last summer, the woman had circled him like a clock hand, broken the rhythm she had long lived by and made her bed wherever she lay with him. She told him about the man whose hands had been burnt raw. He wore velvet gloves, which the woman peeled off him as he slept.

'Hands was the colour of bruised apricots, sure.'

The woman evidently curious to unfold her men, as if they were sheets left to dry out on bushes. Dean smiled. Walter jumped up and rested his forepaws on his shoulders.

'I'm not smiling at you,' he complained, but he wasn't harsh when he set his dog down.

His hand rested on Walter's neck and he felt the pulse crash under his fingers. He remembered the woman crouching to wash herself in a basin of cold water scented with mint leaves. She cleaned herself with the precision of a windscreen wiper: her wet hands moving up her calves and around her buttocks, indifferent to his watching self. She washed away the blood he had drawn from her while making love. He had opened up raw flesh when his nails broke, but instead of apologising had lashed out in his anger, watching her skin flaring up with each blow. Dean tried hunting for the shattered tips of his nails, but they had been lost. He had been lost. He sat and nursed his blunt fingertips and wondered how long it would be before his nails grew again.

The woman had washed herself with a precision that frightened him – no tears, no recriminations. She threw away the mint-scented water and a false eyelash that had landed on her breast, but still she said nothing – even as she walked away. Walter barked at her ankles, anxious, mistrustful. He had seen them plunge and bite, hard and mean. Dean's face had been a bruise for weeks after. He kept to the fields, skirting the campsite, like a hungry fox. He tippy-toed as close as he dared, but he encountered no one. Dean flinched at the memories of what had occurred last summer. In truth, it was still unfinished business. He fingered his bruises with damaged hands and waited.

Winter passed. The fields flooded and it was hard to find a pitch which didn't leave him shivering. Melted ice made jigsaws out of the footpaths running through the Llangybi estate. He ate blackbirds and worms, digging them out with his left hand in order to protect his new nails. He drank melted ice and used it to wash his face. The sharp pang of cold, wet skin. Dean walked in circles to keep his blood spinning through his restless limbs. He broke out of undergrowth thick with frost, his fingers useless in the intense cold. He saw no one for days on end. Walter kept at his heels, yapping for attention, for food, sometimes a warning. Grouse were raised on the estate he robbed of its singing birds. There were CCTV cameras nailed to trees watching him as he circled its parameters. And then one day, one of the estate workers out driving a 4X4 hailed him and offered him a ham baguette.

'SAS, is it? Nod, nod, wink, wink?'

Dean had no idea what the man was on about. He ate the baguette and wiped his mouth with his fingers. The man inspected his growing nails.

'You do coke out here, or what, man?'

A hint, or a question, Dean couldn't tell. It was a long time since he had last talked with anyone – and that had been a disaster. He recalled the woman who had crushed his nails under her ribs: maybe his nails had grown into the scars he had cut in to her back? Dean was vicious with his memory, but shy in conversation with the stranger.

'Guitar.'

'What?'

'I play the guitar. The nails have to be long for that, see.'

Dean stood, hesitant, unsure about the formalities of ending such a conversation. Before he reversed away, the estate man called out:

'You from the campsite? Well, let the bastards know they can have the top field if they keeps the lid on things. All right?'

The 4x4 rocketed out of sight and Dean stood absorbing what he had just heard. Before he left the previous summer, the estate manager had vetoed the travellers' bareback race. The fields by the river where they camped had been marked up by men in white boiler suits. Rumour had it that a new kind of crop was going to be sown on the estate, possibly rape seed. Dean went to sleep at night believing that when he woke up he would be lying in a cloth of gold. It must make more money than potatoes. The woman with the watery hair picked them, her fingernails and jeans cuffed with mud. She cooked the potatoes she stole away in her pockets for their supper.

'Stay with me,' he pleaded.

She hadn't replied, but neither had she run away. Not for a month, or two. The night she broke his nails had been their first – and last – fight. They had locked in silent combat. Her hands were big and raw: their veins marked out like the tubular roots of the potatoes she harvested. There was no breaking her. She bit into his shoulder so hard he fell down on to his knees, crying out with the pain. Blood had seeped up through his denim shirt – tiny circles of blood, like a wee embroidery.

'That'll learn you,' she spat at him.

Dean knew if he returned to the campsite he would

have to face her again, but he also knew he had to pass on news of the estate man's offer. He must go and tell Finn. There was still a chance to get the race organised for the coming summer. Dean made a fire and waited his moment. He waited until nine o'clock for that was when most people would be whiling away the time in their caravans, eating, dozing, making love before night called them into action – Da amongst them. Dean tried to forget about that as he slipped Walter's leash on and made ready to leave. He stamped out the embers of his fire and rolled up his home into a kitbag cut out of an old oilskin. Sleeping bag, portable primus stove, ground sheet, a great coat and some tins of sardines. He tucked the kitbag into a hole he dug under a hedge and made his way down the sloping top field to reach the campsite that stood at its foot.

Nine o'clock. Dean heard the place, before he walked into it: muted voices talking, shouting, arguing, loving. The sound of cups and cutlery rattling through windows propped open with sticks. He walked past window shelves cluttered with china horses and vases of paper flowers, canopied by spools of lace. He knew he would find Finn close to the river. Finn slept in a hammock, rocking himself to sleep listening out for the noise of running water. Dean hurried through the racket and smells made by other people cooking and living. He glimpsed a stooped shadow and, surprised, recognised himself in its hunched contours. He kept one hand free of his coat pocket to muzzle Walter whenever he threatened to bark. Walter was not nervous to be home. He saw old friends everywhere and yearned to make contact again. His tail wagged, his feet skittered sideways and backwards. Dean caught his nose and breathed threats into his floppy ears.

He knocked three times on Finn's door. A year passed, before it was opened. Finn. Five feet and five inches tall, his shoulders broad over a barrel chest and wide-apart legs. He wore a torn polo shirt and Levi's that had probably never seen better days. His face smiled, but his hands hung still, his fists clenched up in to balls.

'Dean?'

'That's me, all right. Can I come in?'

'We didn't think you'd show yet awhile.'

'You thought wrong.'

'No surprises there then.'

'It's okay, is it? I don't want no trouble. I've got a message, see.'

'Look, maybe you should stay away, like? It's still a bit of a hot potato. What happened between you and your old man, an' all.'

Dean not daring to look at Finn, because he wanted to laugh. A hot potato. The woman and her fighting and her stories. She was hot all right. He glanced at Finn.

'She all right, is she?'

'She came back, if that's what you mean.'

Finn turned slowly to face his friend.

'She's here now.'

'With my old man?'

'Yeah. Love's young dream.'

Dean sat down on a stool by the doorway. So, she was back with Da, but was this really such a revelation? She had come back and that's why he had kept away for so long. No, that was not it. He needed to grow his nails and play again. He needed to settle an argument.

'And him?'

'Bastard same as ever he was, Dean. Nose in the trough and what a trough. She's got fat sitting around him.'

'She never has.'

'Aye.'

'It could never have worked, man. She was always his.'

'Well, some things is never going to bastard change. He still wears the gloves.'

'I see.'

'Threatened to get the law on you, he did. We talked him down.'

'He'll never play again.'

Dean thought the weight of his remark might sink Finn's caravan. Finn evidently thought the same, because he quickly changed the subject:

'And what about yourself?'

'I'll play for the rest of my life, if need be, but look, that's not why I'm here, Finn. Saw one of the estate men a few days back and he says we can use the top field for the race, after all.'

'Is that a fact?'

Finn began preparing food for his guest, mulling over the information he had been given. Dean made a study of his place. It was clean, if rather bare. A hammock hung above a deal table. A kitchen unit wrapped round the table, punctuated at each end by two old wicker chairs. Finn opened drawers and cupboard doors and discovered bread, cheese and pickles. Dean ate from reflex, rather than hunger. He could hear movement outside. There were shouted exchanges across the way; doors slammed, windows cracked open.

Snatches of music began to filter through the hessian that Finn had nailed over his windows. Guitars. A drum. A radio. Walter's eager bark. Finn was smiling a broader smile than before.

'Tomorrow, we'll make plans.'

'Tomorrow, I'll go see him, Finn.'

'That wise?'

'Do I have any bastard choice?'

'Always one of those to be made, man.'

'I want to see him.'

'Then want is enough.'

'Does he talk of it ever?'

'Not since Beth came back.'

Finn offered Dean a bottle of beer. They drank slowly and in silence. Finn's hands wrapped round his beer bottle, stiff and awkward where the skin hadn't quite healed. His hands had beaten out the flames Dean started, throwing a match into his Da's outstretched fingers.

They had been wet with tears and petrol. A moment so ugly, he hardly dared think about it now. Hadn't he taken away something that was not his? Worse, he had run. He hadn't faced up to his desires. He slunk away, ashamed and brutal. The woman had followed him. No, he laid a trap and she had fallen into it. He had told so many lies, he could hardly remember a single one of them hours later. Only, that she had come. He had seen her light her way with a cigarette lighter, a small flame edging its way along the field. A wary firefly. Present, she was something huge. Shadows had ringed them. His want of her, the bait that really mattered – no shame, no excuses. They had peeled themselves out of the mud, like Autumn potatoes, careless and random with their mouths and hands. He took, she took. They had been as bad as each other.

'It's him I wants to touch me, Dean,' she confessed. 'He touches me, it will be okay.'

'Stay, Beth.'

'It's not the same when they is under the velvet. It don't feel right.'

Dean realised she was always going to leave him. She was fascinated by what she could not have. He knew that, because he had been the same way himself. He believed he would never have his Da's blessing for taking away the one thing that had always mattered to him. The one thing that bred a jealousy so strong, it choked them both.

'Did you keep my guitar, Finn?'

'I did, Dean boy. On the nail there, behind the door.'

He found it. His fingers hovered over the strings.

'There was never any question you were the better player, Dean. You and his girl, like, that was never the argument you should have had.'

'I'll see him tomorrow, Finn, sure I will.'

'You tell him then what really needs telling, boy. Tomorrow it is. You'll be playing for us, while you're about it, won't you?'

Dean nodded, distracted by thoughts of what might be. Tomorrow – a day of hopes and chances, lit up like beacons. Tomorrow.

Dean found his Da slumped inside a cloud of horsehair stuffing that exploded from a leather armchair. His velvet gloves lay like beautiful wounds on top of the armrests. Dean remembered Da's fingers plucking notes from a guitar, as fast as the raindrops falling outside the caravan. The sounds he made were a cocoon, a challenge, a debate, but all was silent now. His hands were unfamiliar, simply because they were so still. Dean barely glanced at his Da's face. He squatted down, rolled a cigarette and then offered it up to him. Da spat his response, a long, slow arc of spittle that missed its target.

'I'm coming back for the race, Da. It's going to happen, after all. We got the field back.'

There was no reply. Dean tried again.

'I'm going to play later. Will you come and listen?'

Again, there was no reply, but was it just his imagination or did the velvet gloves tremble a little on the armrests?

'I's going to play what you taught me.'

'Tribute hand, is it?'

Da's sarcasm heavier than his punch. Dean rubbed his head, as if hit.

'Nah. I wants to play you something, all right?'

Da slowly lifted up his wounded hands. Beth had sewn large sequins on the ends of the gloves.

'We have to sort this out, Da. Breaking me up, this is. The silence, like. Should never have done what I did, okay? Shit. Never had words I could use proper, like. You and me, we're the same, innit? The music is what counts. Can't never say it right, but put us fingers to the strings . . .'

'You bastard silenced me. Can't never forgive you that. The woman is nothing, all said and done, is she? Circles me like some bastard cat does a cringing bird it's going to kill. Always taking a peek here and there under the gloves. Is this a life, I ask you?'

'You should never have tried stopping me.'

Da placed his hands back down on the armrests in slow motion. Dean suddenly thought of a melody that would capture his strange, gentle gesture. He tapped it against his boot with his newly grown nails.

'Thought you'd be proud of me, Da, wanting to take on the music an' all. A credit to you, yeah? But what did you really think? Whittle me down to a splinter, was that it? Make me not count and you still the big man? Not no more. It was always going to happen, whatever I did. Not that I'm saying it's an excuse, mind, but you pushed me. On and on with your tricks and lies. Cheated me of my gigs, even my songs. Couldn't see anyone better than you stand up there on race nights and play for the crowd. Leastways, could never see your son up there.'

A small rustle behind Dean's head alerted him to Beth's presence. She had been resting on the ledge that hung over the stove. He caught a glimpse of her sweaty cheeks and sleep-loose lips. Beth yawned and pushed back her wing of dyed red hair. A bare white leg slipped out from under the blanket. Naked and not caring. Dean didn't care, either. He turned back to Da. His long grey hair was caught up in an elastic band and it was thinner than he remembered. Da's face had sunk in too, as if two fists had punched into a ball of dough. His lips were pale and chapped, the eyes the only point of recognition. They were almost black in this light, although really they were a dapple grey, the colour of the Welsh cob he used to ride in the bareback races as a boy.

'What you say, Da?'

'Going to shake my bastard hand?'

Da spat out his self-pity, like he had just invented a new kind of bomb. Beth sat immobile on the bed. Her freckled breasts hung low, her hands gripped her knees.

'I want us to go to the race together.'

'A united front?'

'Father and son. Is that so bastard hard to remember?'

'I remember, boy. I remember pain so bad my skin turned into melted bone.'

'I is sorry, Da. Thought I'd be remembering you right learning to play, like you did . . .'

'Lost me everything and he wants to snuggle down and play happy families. You hearing this, Beth, lovely? You want cuckoo-boy-in-the-nest living here again?'

Beth rigid with tension – or might it be curiosity? Dean stared at his Da's sunken face, watching his lips moving but not always clear about the words coming from them.

'Makes his bed, lies in it. Lies in a good many others too. What you saying, Beth? Can't hear you none. Speak up. Bastard speak up!'

'Nothing to say, Padraig. Actions speak louder than words.'

'I'll play us a tune then, is it?'

'That's not never going to happen now, is it, bach?'

Beth advanced on Da. Her hands cupped his face. Da buried his face in Beth. She presented Dean with her naked back. Embarrassed, he stared instead at Da's hands in their green velvet gloves. Green. The colour of jealousy. The colour of Spring. Dean left the caravan. He sat down on the steps outside and smoked the cigarette his father had refused earlier. It was quiet inside. He thought he could hear Beth's whisperings, but he wasn't sure. Dean threw the butt away and stood up. It was nearly eleven o'clock. There were a few people making the rounds. Women from the site were hanging out their washing. A few of them took a second look when they recognised him, but no one said anything. The whole world seemed to balance itself on his Da's steps: one step to the left, one step to the right, it would all come tumbling down like Humpty Dumpty falling off his wall. Dean waited. He heard a woman's footsteps behind him, something sharp and pointed, like a stiletto heel. Dean turned round and there was Beth, wrapped in a blanket, her feet shod in apple-red ankle boots.

'I's talked to him, Dean. He's hurting bad, but it's not just his hands. He knows he done wrong too, but he won't be saying it out loud. How can he? It's not his way. I's going to try again, later. You go on to Finn's. I'll get him to come out for you. He's proud, that's what it is. You both are, all said and done. Like father, like bastard son.'

Beth smiled. Her lips were stained with something pink. There was a faint smell of onions and juniper when she spoke to him up close. Her smile was her best feature, in spite of her decayed teeth. Her smile spoke her generosity, her forgiveness. She was back with Padraig Cafferty, after all. She didn't want trouble, anymore than he did.

'You do what you can, I'll be grateful, Beth. Can't expect no bloody miracles, can I, now?'

'Oh, I don't know, lovely. Something of a miracle you has turned up at all. Didn't never expect that, truth told.'

'Maybe that's the problem: you hopes for too much, you can never be happy.'

'I's got to get back to him, bach. Wish me luck.'

Beth slammed the door behind him, but it was for effect only. Dean walked back to Finn's, expectation rising in him in spite of what he had just claimed. It was like yeast piling into his veins. By the time he got to Finn's, he was full of optimism for the evening ahead. He knew Macready the Fiddler was travelling down from Merthyr to play with him – Finn had received a text message to that effect only that morning – and there would be many other drummers and guitarists anxious to get a chance to play with Dean Cafferty, son of the legendary Padraig Cafferty. His father had once played a marathon thirty-hour session, letting his fingers bleed on to his strings. This was the man Dean remembered so strongly that it was a shock to think back to the encounter in the caravan with the diminished man that was his father, disguised by his Alvin Stardust gloves.

Dean felt himself fill when he thought about the velvet gloves. He could see Finn playing with Walter on the grass outside his caravan and he hurriedly wiped away his tears. He couldn't be weak, not now. Dean joined in Finn's game. They teased Walter by hiding a knotted rope behind their backs, which he was anxious to sink his teeth into. Finn kept his questions to himself, until they got back inside the caravan and opened up some cans.

'Well, then, Dean?'

'She says she's going to get him out, tonight. She's determined on it.'

'He's got no chance then. He'll be there.'

Tonight.

Expectation coiled in Dean's stomach. Tonight, his guilt trapped in his throat, along with all the words left unspoken for too long. Tonight, was going to be a small miracle. He couldn't walk away again, even if Da willed him to go with all that was left of his strength. The improvised stage where he was to play was nothing more than a piece of grass lying beneath two old trees. Their branches had grown into each other to provide a natural canopy over the musicians. Players came and went, but the audience waited impatiently for one man. Dean felt their expectancy crowd him, so he took his time tuning his guitar in Finn's caravan. He tightened his strings up to such a pitch, he felt they might echo the shriek of a struck match landing in an upturned palm.

The music he played was as fierce. It was a flame licking bone and skin; it was a woman's curiosity, peeling back emotions of despair and jealousy, as threadbare as old sheets. The progression of Dean's melodies bit into each other like noisy packs of street dogs. He played and applause ripped through the air, loud and harsh. Catcalls, whistles. His set finished, he caught sight of Beth hovering by the trees. She was reluctant to step on to the stage. He smiled reassurance. Eventually, she made the journey over the outstretched legs and discarded beer bottles that ringed the stage. She stopped in front of him, reaching into her pockets as she did so. She pulled out the sequin gloves. They looked jaunty, but they were a rebuff all the same.

'Sorry,' Beth said.

'Pride comes after the fall, is what it is.'

Dean leant down and picked up the gloves. He knew there would be no point trying them on for size. There were some things he could never match.

EGG SPELLS

Lizzie's dislocated eyeballs rested in the palm of his hand. They were the consistency of two softly boiled eggs. Maximilian carefully scrutinised each of the eyes, before dropping them gently on to the silver tray by his elbow. They looked so bald without their lashes.

She had been fifteen when he had met her on the Gower sands. He watched her chase the wind into the sea and discover the corpse of a dog on the tide. Its pelt had been reduced to a hideous waxiness and the black pits of its eye sockets filled with pebbles. He stepped in after her and cupped his hands against her face. That was the first time he had felt her eyelashes brush against his fingers. Later, Lizzie Morgan told him that she lived on the beaches that fringed his estate. She ate raw birds' eggs, plucked from nests hidden in the salt-dry rushes of the shoreline. The day they found the dog, dried egg yolk had lain like a crust of frost across her right cheek. The sight of Lizzie's stained face prompted Maximilian to ask her to marry him.

His tenants were shocked. They knew Lizzie Morgan to be as daft as a spoon, but then there was no fool like an old fool. Maximilian knew he was old – particularly when he tried to run and keep up with a hanged man's daughter – but once he started running after her, he couldn't stop. He couldn't stop now. Maximilian shifted Lizzie's new glass eyes between his curled fingers. They clicked together as he spun them around, faster and faster.

– I could knock the eyes out of your bastard head! So I could.

– Sorry, sorry, sorry.

– Everybody's always sorry, but it's always too late. Poor dog. But I'm hungry now. Will you buy me food, sir?

– Everything you could ever want, Lizzie.

– Will I wear a white dress in church?

– If you like. Do you love me, Lizzie Morgan?

– I don't know.

Lizzie had never known very much about anything, unless she could bite into it very hard and taste it, raw and unscented. She chewed up meals and titbits, like a hungry wolf. Her teeth were slightly yellow and very crooked, but they were strong. Maximilian screamed when she bit into his thigh and drew blood as they made love for the first time. It was the night after the day they found the dog on the beach and he proposed to her as she stood sheltering behind his hands. Lizzie's teeth carved into his body. She quite literally seemed to feed on him. Her incredible appetites – both inside and outside the tapestried sanctity of the four-poster bed –

revolted and shocked the household servants. But Maximilian de St Blaize adored his Lizzie.

He refused to alter a stitch of her dress, or improve a single one of her unpredictable manners. The neighbouring gentry avoided his company, but Lizzie seemed oblivious of their contempt of her. She stretched herself out on the long dining table in the hall of her new home and chewed away at the strips of beef, which her husband wrapped around his hands to feed her. He teased and tormented her, like he did one of his hunting hawks, hiding the food she desired until she appeared tamed and yielding, fresh for his plunder. Lizzie boasted the russet and cream colouring of a prize pheasant and she was as plump as a quail.

Like a bird, her instinct was to run for cover whenever strangers appeared, but she faced Maximilian down when he stood before her on the shoreline and asked her her name. Unconcerned by his crushed velvet-and-lace-elegance, she wiped away the egg yolk dribbling down from the corners of her mouth and smiled up at him. Maximilian saw a vision – his heart pounded itself into a strange kind of fury. He would snatch up this strange jewel from the sands and run away with her to prevent another sharing in her dirty glory.

– *Lizzie Morgan, sir. That's my name, see. Baptised over there in the church with the green slate roof. And there was a special cake made me. But I couldn't eat then, I couldn't.*

– You have been eating eggs, recently, I think.
– I eats them here. I'm all day long running, see.
– I do see, Lizzie Morgan.

He saw nothing but Lizzie Morgan. He pinned her against him, like a watch chain, and refused to acknowledge the outrage of his friends. After the outbreak of the war against Napoleon, they went to market to oversee the sale of his prize sheep. He marvelled at her lack of self-consciousness. She straddled the bars of the pens in the auction rooms, revealing legs bare of any coverings, except her own golden hair. In the tavern, she tore at her meat and potatoes with her hands, before stopping to clean them against the folds of her old print frock.

In the Autumn following their marriage, she discovered an extraordinary emporium that had opened in the High Street of the nearby market town.

– There is strange creatures in there, like the ones sewn on the bed curtains. A Noah's Ark of a shop, to be sure.

Lizzie handed him a pamphlet she had found on the street outside the shop and he read it out to her:

'The knowledge of my secrets I have gathered in my travels abroad (where I have spent my time ever since I was fifteen years old to this, my nine and twentieth year) in France and Italy and in the Dark Continents. Those that have travelled to these places might tell you what a miracle of art I have achieved to assist Nature in the preservation of her own Great works. In my

shop, bear witness to the following marvels: Two Elephant heads can be seen attached to giant wooden shields. From each of their Ivory tusks, swings a Monkey; below their bald feet, two Leopards paw the ground, Pythons coiled, like a ladies stole, around their necks.

Two giant Turtles do walk at the heels of these rare beasts, each one ridden by three white Owls. These are the sights I promise you, I, Silas Trotter, gentlemen and trader in Exotic Species. Therefore be not unwilling to come, but suspend your Judgment till you have try'd and then speak as you find.'

– *Can I have a leopard?*

– *Why a leopard?*

– *They look like they can run as fast as me.*

Lizzie Morgan's hands were as quick and agile as her running legs. She could steal eggs from under a mother hen's beak and she could spin yarn as fine as the floating seeds of a clock flower. Her hands traced Maximilian's tired, old body, like two jittery lacewings. She was a warm, living clod of a body, curled into his shoulder at night under the family's dusty heraldic trappings. Chilled by draughts and doubts, Maximilian fed on her blood-red heat. He felt his old heart tick with anticipation as she breathed against him – strong, regular breaths. He counted them under his own short breaths when he couldn't sleep. When Lizzie died, the palms of her hands had turned up, as if in resignation at what lay before her. She died from a tumour that had grown in her left breast. Her last breaths were ugly and hoarse. Maximilian plugged his ears with animal fat so that he could not hear her die, but her upturned palms told their own story. They flipped over like spun coins and the deed was done. Lizzie was just seventeen the day she died.

Maximilian mourned his wife, like one possessed. The six cooks employed in the kitchens were instructed to bake her favourites foods. They were set out on big silver serving dishes to form a culinary garland around her black marble bier in the Great Hall. Maximilian wandered through the fifty rooms of his house, catching glimpses of his wife's discarded clothing. He thought momentarily that she must have come in from the sea and thrown off her clothes to dry out by one of the many fires they kept burning throughout the day. But then he remembered Lizzie's cold body lying in state on the dining room table. Maximilian had also grown very cold since his wife had died. He couldn't stay warm, even when sitting in the inglenook fireplaces in the Great Hall. No heat could warm him, like Lizzie's hands and breath had done, and he missed her. Her empty skirts and bodices were all he had to fill out the hollow of his new life. He shook out the folds of her dresses and breathed up their eggy-perfumed smell. In the folds of her old print frock, he discovered the pamphlet advertising *Trotter's Emporium for Exotic Species*. The seeds of a new obsession were sown as he once again read his way through Silas Trotter's manifesto. Here was a man, who like the Bible's Noah, preferred to work in twos. Maximilian, deprived of his other half, found himself drawn by curiosity to visit his premises.

He discovered Silas Trotter inside his shop, an alligator slung across his shoulder, like a flitch of bacon. The taxidermist could see from the cut of Maximilian's suit that he was a rich man, but he was also a much troubled man. The pouches under his bloodshot eyes were grey and heavy with tiredness. Silas pulled out an old armchair and gestured to his esteemed visitor to make himself comfortable. Maximilian was wearing a black velvet coat so his armband of mourning wasn't immediately visible to the taxidermist.

'A recent bereavement, sir?'

'Just a day since, my wife, my dear wife passed away . . .'

Maximilian felt the tears start in his eyes. He hurried up from the armchair in order to avoid the other man's intense gaze. There was no escaping the fact that the taxidermist's eyes were as hard and as unyielding as those of his stuffed animals. Maximilian felt uncomfortable, but not because of the reference made to his armband. There was something else that worried him about the crowded, fusty interior of *Trotter's Emporium for Exotic Species*. It was the sense of being surrounded by dead flesh that nevertheless seemed to have a life of its own.

Wherever he turned his attention, Maximilian found himself face to face with eyes that glinted in the half-lit shop interior, like dozens of tiny ebony beads. A large quantity of horseshoe bats hung from the ceiling's wooden beams, like bunches of dried herbs; below their caped wings, foxes and stoats prowled across the floorboards. Suddenly, Maximilian felt a draught blow through the room, as if all the animals had together taken a sharp intake of breath and exhaled in memory of the deceased woman.

'My heartfelt condolences, dear sir. I, too, lost my wife to a terrible fever, just two years ago. There was nothing to be done, nothing.'

Hearing this, Maximilian swung round on his toes and interrupted his host.

'Nothing, sir? Death is a foe, like one of your foxes here when he chased a farmer's hens. Nothing more, nothing less. He must be challenged and not ignored. You see that for yourself, as I can judge from your shop's wares. All of these creatures once lived and breathed, but then you took their dead bodies and you restored them. They have not been left to rot in a grave, to lose all that once made them alive in the eyes of the world around them.'

Silas had an acute sense of smell, vital if he were to check for any unfortunate leakages in his sales goods. But this time he smelled something different – *something out of the ordinary run of things*. He had not, of course, built up his extraordinary operation through coy diffidence. Silas had never known what it was to stand in a shadow. He ached for a spotlight and he invariably found one.

He was a showman and a conjuror – *now you see it, now you don't, ladies and gentlemen.* Death treading his remorseless path, but then sidetracked with a flick of a scalpel, wielded with the accuracy of a duellist; or the cluster of brain cells teased out of the nostril with a hooked taper that might put you in mind of Casanova toying with an oyster.

'It is possible, dear sir, to preserve human flesh and not just that of an animal.'

Maximilian took another look around the shop and encountered the watchful ebony eyes of the foxes, stoats and alligators parading its floorboards. How well they· simulated Nature, even in the frozen poses of Death. The fox standing by his right foot looked as if it could take flight the moment a pack of hounds were scented at his brushy tail. Beside the fox was a stoat, who lurched upwards on its hind legs, a bamboo frame large enough to take the weight of a gentleman's top hat clasped between its front paws. Maximilian mopped his brow with his pocket handkerchief.

'If you were to carry out such an operation, sir, I must ask of you one favour.'

'Name it.'

Silas now scented the whiff of victory, over and above the acrid stink of the oil he had used to clean down the alligators' skins. He smiled and Maximilian, still in awe of the many clawed spectators around him, visibly started on catching sight of his very white, very real-looking teeth so close to his own living eyes. Silas seeing his shocked expression explained that he had filed them down from the rescued fragments of a broken porcelain basin.

'What you see, dear sir, is not always what you expect. A lesson in life's mysteries, I think. But your request?'

'That I attend the operation throughout. Please.'

Silas chewed on his porcelain teeth for some minutes whilst he absorbed this plea. No other client had ever asked to attend an embalming before and he was temporarily at a loss for words. Certain aspects of his profession were of necessity shrouded in secrecy. He was a hunter, a smuggler, a man who contravened the very basic laws of Nature, let alone the tenets of Christianity. He brought back the dead and he traded their corpses for profit. *A stitch in time, and a fortune is mine* was this man's motto. Silas Trotter was a name that a small band of cognoscenti recognised and admired, but many others flinched with horror when they heard he was loose in their midst. Luckily, the widower Maximilian had only one point of reference: his dead Lizzie. He thought of her now lying unattended amongst dozens of plates of uneaten delicacies and wept loudly, unrestrained by the presence of the stranger seated beside him.

'I beg you, sir. Meet my request. Think of your own dear wife.'

'She is with me still, dear sir.'

Silas leered and tapped at his set of porcelain teeth.

'It was her sink, dear sir, which I smashed to pieces. I am not one to show emotion as a rule, but I was driven to distraction when she made a particularly bad deal over some tigers. *Marjory Postlethwaite, you are a damned fool*, I cried. *You Sir*, she had replied, *will eat my words one day*. Which I suppose I do whenever I have occasion to quote her, God rest her soul. She was not, you understand, much in the way of a business woman. I, on the other hand, excel at my trade. I accept your commission. And what a tribute to the lady's beauty, dear sir. That you intend creating a portrait unlike any other to remember her by. I salute such appreciation of my art, as well, of course, evidence of your great passion and devotion.'

Silas shook his head and then Maximilian shook his hand. It was long and lean with five beautifully manicured nails, each topped with a neat, white half-moon. They were not what he expected from a man who dealt with jars of obnoxious poisons. Maximilian shuddered, stepped back and stumbled over the hat-bearing stoat.

'You will come to my house this evening, sir. There can be no delay.'

Saying this, Maximilian gathered up his hat, gloves and stick and exited *Trotter's Emporium for Exotic*

Species. His brain stung with what he had heard, seen and inhaled during the past four hours. Yes, four hours had passed since he stepped through Trotter's doorway. He checked his pocket watch and read its dial with a sense of shock. It seemed in this encounter that his initial terror at Lizzie's abandonment of him had been transformed into a rare kind of courage. He had succeeded in making a bargain with a man, who tinkered with Life and Death as if they were no more than a pair of suspect cogs in the workings of a run-down carriage clock. Could it really be that simple to reverse the accepted order of things? After all, he was a man who went to church on Sunday, because he had always gone to church on Sunday. He ate beef, because he had always eaten beef. He wore dubbined boots of leather and took snuff, because that was the custom. He became a magistrate and then a member of Parliament for a very rotten Borough, because that was expected of him. Then one day he caught sight of a girl with an egg-smeared face, her hands full of broken shells, whom he married a week after he signed her father's death warrant. So, he discovered happiness at the grand old age of fifty nine. It was possible, he was now convinced, to restore such an emotion – even in the face of death.

Maximilian put away his watch and beckoned to his coachman, whom he had ordered to wait for him in a discreet backstreet. He arrived home in good time, but still Silas had somehow managed to reach the mansion in advance of his host, complete with two, very large leather holdalls. They rattled loudly as they were hauled up the entrance steps and into the the library where the taxidermist was installed to begin work on his unique portrait of a dead lady. The stranger issued his instructions and the Baronet obeyed, much to the incredulity of his servants. He had the long deal table brought up from the kitchen, along with several big basins and trays. After several hours of furniture shifting and candle lighting, the library door was shut closed on the two men and a deep silence reigned within for the next twenty-four hours.

What thoughts came into Maximilian's mind as Silas made the first incision into his wife's naked body? The initial cut ran from her sternum to the bottom of her navel as she opened up like a soft leather purse in the embalmer's long yellow fingers. Maximilian stood by his side throughout the operation, mesmerised at the revelation of his wife's inner workings, moulded in their folds of muscle and tissue. This was the essence of his dear Lizzie? A pile of wet intestines? The stubby pulp of a heart severed from its fleshy home? He felt fascinated by the intricate webs of nerve and sinew he saw stretched out before him. Not even the sound of Silas' careful stitching, drawing together the loose flaps of his wife's skin, could shock him. The taxidermist was unquestionably a craftsman of the highest order. He worked with great grace, looping cat-gut thread into his needles and then knotting up its ends beneath the

115

folds of Lizzie's white skin. Her diseased breast was removed and replaced with a leather counterfeit stuffed with straw, then he plied his needle in a series of herringbone stitches, working his way up Lizzie's unbreathing chest. Finally, her hollow eye sockets were filled with the glass replicas that Maximilian had carried around the house with him in the quiet hours of early morning. A pair of blue eyes – as blue as the bird eggs Lizzie had once gorged on the shoreline.

'They looked so bald without eyelashes, but now..'

'You will retire, sir, whilst I add the finishing touches,' Silas said gently.

He could see that Maximilian was overwhelmed at the sight of his new glass-eyed Lizzie. She did indeed look a little fresher, although the air in the library stank of the evidence of her unnatural preservation order. Silas dressed her in the white frock she had worn in church for her wedding. It was as loose and fine as the membrane of an egg. Then he painted her face in a light coating of cosmetics. A touch of powder and rouge and some cochineal paste for her lips.

'Now, lady, you are ready,' Silas whispered into her cold ear.

He folded her hands across her breasts with great delicacy, as if trying to prevent her from waking, and then blew out the candles that stood too close to the body. In the softer light, Lizzie Morgan did indeed look as if she had just fallen asleep. Silas smiled. His genius was reflected in her glass eyes, which, thanks to the subdued lighting, had lost their shiny, manufactured surface. He stepped to the door and called out to the baronet before withdrawing into the corridor.

Maximilian stood hesitantly in the doorway. It was only a short distance to the kitchen table, but those few yards worked a most miraculous effect, easing out the more obvious signs of Lizzie's true state. He shuffled forwards, almost afraid to look upon her. He paused by her feet, which were still bare, and marvelled at what he finally allowed himself to see: Lizzie's cheeks glowed again, as they had on the shoreline. Her eggshell blue eyes reflected the lights around her and they seemed as alive as they had ever been. Maximilian reached into his coat pocket and drew out a small bird's egg. Picking up one of the empty bowls left by the table, he cracked it open, careful to keep its yolk unbroken. Then he dipped his fingers into the egg and tenderly stroked them down the side of his wife's face.

'You have been eating eggs, recently, I think, Lizzie Morgan?'

KISSING CALICO

'The trick is to begin with a solution, then work backwards.'

This was the advice Crawley Hughes gave to Maisie Thomas when he began to teach her mathematics in his kitchen in Cathedral Road. She didn't know of very many solutions, however, and so had to improvise from memory.

'You mean, like: love and marriage equals a horse and carriage, sir?'

Crawley Hughes laughed, but they persevered. Maisie thought she would never get the hang of sums, but her employer made them seem nothing more threatening than the ordered steps of a favourite dance – each had its place in the scheme of things. The next step was to learn to tell the time. Crawley Hughes could make the seasons change by turning the hands on his gilt-pocket watch. Maisie watched his fingers turn time on its head.

'Out with the old, in with the new, girlie.'

The pocket watch rode next to her employer's pinstriped trouser leg. He had once let her hold that watch, so Maisie could see for herself how its hands were turned. It was a beautiful watch, shiny as the knives she had to polish every day. Having been resting against his leg, its gold case was as hot as her breath. She returned the watch to Crawley Hughes. His waiting hands were like shovels. The hair from his arm coursed down to the tips of his fingers. Maisie wanted to stroke them, like she did the fur on a cat. He pulled a chair up close to her in the kitchen as she recited her times tables and she sensed the heat he gave off, fiercer than the fire in the grate by her toes. Crawley Hughes always wore his sleeves rolled up, even in the coldest of weathers.

It had been cold when Maisie arrived at the house in Cathedral Road, anxious to find out about a situation advertised in the evening Echo for a 'maid of all work'.

'Will there be food, Mam?'

'Will you let off whining, Maisie. You have to be grown up now.'

'But will there be food?'

Maisie was terrified of getting lost in the big three-storey house with nothing to eat. One day, Crawley Hughes saw her lift an apple from the fruit bowl in the dining room. He winked and pointed upstairs. Up above their heads, his wife Myrtle lay coughing.

'Nothing said, and you get fed, girlie.'

Maisie blushed. Later, she threw the apple away into the boating lake in the little park she visited on her rare days off. It was not that she felt bad about stealing the apple; she hadn't liked the air of complicity that had grown up between her and Crawley Hughes. After the apple incident, he seemed always to show up wherever she was working, even in the remotest of corners. Maisie came to feel that he was watching over her.

'I'm not a thief, sir. Please. I won't do it no more.'

'You will not do what anymore, girlie?'

'Take food.'

'You're hungry?'

'Yes.'

'Then take what you need. After all, Mrs Hughes rarely eats these days. Take her share.'

Maisie eventually learnt to tell the time by watching the hands move on Crawley Hughes' pocket watch, but there were other ways of keeping time. In winter, she stripped green apple wood with her bare hands and fed the sticks into the big kitchen grange, whilst in spring, she washed the window nets free from the soot of smoking fires. In the summer, Maisie cleaned the cutlery outside, because she could see then just how good she was when she spun her blades up into the glaring sunlight. When winter next came round, Maisie would warm herself up by plunging her bare arms into the washing coppers. Any sheets left hanging outside for too long had to be doused with boiling water from a kettle. Maisie hopped from foot to foot in the snow and sang little bits of songs that she had learnt at school whilst she unfroze the bed sheets.

She liked the summer months best of all. Once summer officially arrived – and it was only official after Crawley Hughes reset his watch – Maisie could abandon her hat. She could walk down to the corner bakery without her thin serge coat on. She could see the blossoms out on the trees in front of the old synagogue and she could catch the sound of birds in the nearby park, which had a boating lake, a hothouse and hundreds of flowers. Each bed of flowers came with a little name tag, written in a funny language which she tried hard to decipher as she dug her bare toes into the park grass.

Myrtle Hughes had once owned a draper's shop nearby. The baker had revealed this to Maisie one day. Three months after coming back from honeymoon, Mrs Hughes had retired to her bed and, as far as he could tell, had not emerged from under her quilt since. Her husband did everything for her and Maisie knew that part of his tale to be true. She had been ordered never to enter Myrtle's bedroom. She occasionally walked into Crawley Hughes room on the opposite side of the landing to place a stone water bottle at the foot of his bed. It was the size of a box room. The walls were brown, the floor uncarpeted, and the bed as narrow as her own upstairs in the attic. Maisie found this arrangement intriguing. Her parents slept in a giant-sized bed, which took up nearly the entire floor of their bedroom in the family home in Zinc Street. It was a perilously big place for young children to get themselves lost in, all mysterious curves and dips and the odd loose spring. When she was little, Maisie and her five older sisters spent a lot of time ferreting their way into their parents' bed. It was their favourite adventure. Maisie had always slept best curled up between her parents. She was finally weaned from this habit when she turned nine.

'It's not the done thing anymore, Maisie, lovely. Out you go now.'

Her mother shooed her out of bed and from that day onwards she had felt like an overcurious pigeon, pathetically hopping around for scraps of affection. Lying in exile on really cold winter nights, Maisie had to breathe over her own sheets in an attempt to warm them – but it was only an echo of the heat that had emanated from her parents' bed. Since leaving them, Maisie had always felt the cold. Only the hottest of suns persuaded her to roll up her sleeves and abandon her hat. Maisie was tiny – her Mam said she had no flesh on her to keep in the heat.

'Pocket size, pocket wise,' her father joked.

This comment puzzled Maisie. What more did she need to know about the contents of pockets? Pockets were places where you kept loose change, handkerchiefs, ticket stubs and sweets. But they could also be places of deep mystery, her father suggested. When Crawley Hughes first set his watch before her and she saw how it captured time with its tiny gold hands, she wondered if this might not be the mystery her father had been alluding to.

'Is Mrs Hughes really ill, sir? Is she at death's door?'

Crawley Hughes laughed at her question.

'If she is, he's in need of a bloody loud door knocker! Excuse me, Maisie, but Mrs Hughes has been something of a *trial* during our married life. Her illnesses are well . . . not real ones. There are difficulties in the way she sees things, compared to say, how we see things.'

'Can she do the maths right?'

'She can calculate, certainly, Maisie.'

Mr Hughes put his hands together behind his head and leant back in his chair. *Summer was a-coming in . . .* Summer. Maisie left off wearing her hat and she rolled down her stockings. The sun was beginning to burn through her skin and into her bones. She found herself skipping and running when she visited the park. Winter was gone. Winter. You watched winter unfold in the light given out by candles and fire flames. Summer was light in itself. Maisie polished the chairs in the front room until they shone like the sun outside. She could see the chair legs reflected in the parquet floor. Her hands bled from her efforts. She wrapped them up in loose pieces of calico, the ones not going to be used to boil puddings on a Sunday, and hugged them to her as she sat out her evenings in the kitchen.

Mr Hughes saw her bandaged hands one night. He asked whether there had been an accident? And Maisie said, no, it was the cleaning that did it. You need a servant, girlie, he replied. They both laughed. Mr Hughes was in his shirtsleeves as usual, pushing out heat like a small furnace. Maisie began crying. She had no idea why, but it was something to do with his body heat and his kindness, all mixing in together with her unspent tears. Maisie hadn't really had a good cry since she was kicked out of her parents' bed.

'The sheets, they was so cold. And I was on my own, sir . . . and God, what am I saying . . . sorry, sir.'

Mr Hughes reached into his pocket for a handkerchief and handed it over to Maisie.

'I didn't think you were unhappy, Maisie. I hear you singing out here. And once, in the park, you know, I saw you skip across the grass. Not a care in the world, I thought.'

Maisie tried hard to think of what her particular cares might be, but try as she might she could not put her finger on any one reason for her tears.

'It's like that sometimes, isn't it, sir? It all seems as black as the grate down there. You don't know what will happen next.'

'Yes, that's very true, Maisie. Now, you must give me your word that when you next feel like the inside of that grate, you will tell me? I don't like to think of you crying down here, all alone.'

He turned away from her. Maisie wondered if he often thought of her. She found the idea strange and exciting all at once. She assumed nobody really thought about her very much, not even her own family. They were so busy squabbling and shouting and laughing and drinking.

'Get off the sidings, and step on the main track.'

'Stop joking me, Da. Please.'

Maisie's father was a signalman on the railways. He made trains stop and start, pulling levers and pressing switches. He made things happen all the time. Maisie was not like that, she never had been; she had always stood firmly on the sidings in spite of her father's exhortations to move on. The main track meant being fast enough to keep up and Maisie had never been one for keeping up. She thought about her abysmal attempts to learn her times tables at school. Mr Hughes moved towards the kitchen door. He turned before he left and smiled at her. Maisie smiled back.

Autumn came and went in a flurry of wet leaves and chillblained fingertips. Maisie shivered when she stepped into the house from the cold streets outside. Mr Hughes lent her his sheepskin gloves one day. They were huge, but her fingers burnt like toast in their grasp. The leather gloves had moulded themselves to fit round Mr Hughes' hands. She could sense them wrapped round her own fingers when she slipped her hands deep down inside her pockets. *Pocket size, pocket wise.* She was wise about very little, but she felt she was slowly learning something very important.

From that day onwards, Mr Hughes always lent her his gloves. She tried returning them when she got back from her walk in the park, but he would put them back inside her pockets and pat her sides and then one day, his hands had stayed still on her hips. The furry hands with their square topped fingers. Maisie shivered, but she wasn't cold. Mr Hughes was only a few inches taller than her and she found herself on a level with his chin. Looking up, she could see into his eyes. His hands were warm on her hips. She placed her own hands on top of his.

'See, sir. They is as warm as yours is now.'

'My name, Maisie, is Crawley. Will you call me Crawley?'

'Yes, sir . . . Crawley..'

'Knighted by a lady. How fitting.'

He kissed her forehead and withdrew his hands. Maisie was disappointed. She wanted him to go on holding her. She kept her hands on her hips as she retreated into the kitchen. She was slow, but she was not stupid. Her sisters told her in soft whispers what they did with the men they picked up at the cafes in Broadway. Maisie giggled and then she laughed out loud. No. 'Goings on' happened best in beds like the one in Zinc Street, with its hot sheets and its loose springs. Maisie had always felt safe in that bed. She wondered if Mr Hughes – if Crawley – would expect her to lie down with him on his bed in the box room? Did she want to lie down with him? She rather thought she would. She jumped up and rescued his gloves from her coat pockets. Slowly, she drew them over her fingers, smoothing over their cracks, thinking all the while of Crawley Hughes' hairy-tipped fingers resting on her hips.

She removed the gloves and hoisted her dress up, laying her fingers against her hip bone to check again the sensation of skin on skin. What did she feel? Just the warm touch of her fingers, nothing else. She didn't feel the same sensation she had experienced when Crawley let his hands rest on her body. She slowly stroked her hips. Her skin was calico-pale, her stomach soft and slightly rounded. She pulled her dress and slip up even further in order to stroke her stomach. Maisie pushed the palms of her hands down against her stomach and looked up – Mr Hughes was standing in the kitchen doorway watching her.

Neither of them moved for what seemed like an age. Maisie's hands stayed exactly where they were. She caught her breath. Mr Hughes seemed to turn around, but then he was crossing the floor towards her. Maisie's heart thumped so hard, she thought it might jump out of her chest. He knelt down before her and gently removed her hands from her stomach. Then he kissed her, twice, on her belly button before getting back up and leaving the kitchen. Maisie's dress slipped back down over her stomach. Her own hands were left hanging in mid-air. When his lips touched the soft skin of her stomach, she had felt the strange shivering start up again.

Winter. Cold and dank, but Myrtle Hughes' coughing fits seemed to have abruptly stopped. The Saturday after the kiss in the kitchen, Maisie heard her coughing fit to burst. Then all had been quiet, very quiet. The silence continued all day Sunday. Mr Hughes did not come down into the parlour to eat any of his meals. He asked for them to be delivered up to his box bedroom, and she hardly glimpsed him at all. He asked not to be disturbed. Her half-day was scheduled for Monday that week, but she had gone out reluctantly. The park was very cold. When she returned home, Mr Hughes was waiting in the hallway for her.

'My wife has died, Maisie. It was very sudden in the end. Shortly after you left the house. The doctor has been and he has told me she suffered very little.'

'Will there be a funeral, sir?'

'On Wednesday. At her family home in Scunthorpe. I shall have to travel up.'

He left her then and went into the parlour. She heard him shut the door and that was that for the rest of the day. Maisie sat alone in the kitchen and wondered why everything felt so strange. She thought she might go and ask Mr Hughes whether he wanted something to eat, but he came into the kitchen and cancelled his own supper. He briefly pulled her to him, guiding her head to rest against his stomach. He was what Maisie's mother would describe as *'being on the portly side.'* His belly was as soft as the bed in Zinc Street. Maisie burrowed up against him. Her hands found their way to his waist, which she squeezed as hard as she could in what she hoped was a sympathetic gesture. She felt clumsy touching him. Mr Hughes caught up her hands after a few minutes and returned them to her lap.

'Sleep tight, dear heart. I have things to do.'

Then he was gone. Maisie felt his body heat still radiating across the kitchen. She hugged her arms across her chest and tried to imagine they were Mr Hughes' arms. She wanted to be held tight as she slept.

On the morning of Myrtle's funeral, Crawley disappeared out of the front door bearing two large suitcases. Returning home the following morning, he asked Maisie if she would like to go on holiday.

'I don't know, Crawley. I've never had a holiday before. Do you mean the seaside?'

Maisie pictured herself riding on a donkey, with Crawley at her side feeding her strawberries and cream. Her fifteenth birthday was just days away. Maybe they would celebrate by eating dinner in a hotel?

'No. A real holiday. We have to go on a ship. It's more of an adventure, Maisie. Something to help me forget the past.'

'I suppose so. Can I tell me Mam?'

'Not necessary. We'll only be gone for a week or two. She can't miss you in that short space of time now, can she?'

Maisie returned to the kitchen to prepare lunch. She was excited at the thought of sailing for the first time, but she was also worried. How was she going to pay for anything? And besides, what did you wear on a boat? Crawley laughed off her worries.

'We shall make do, Maisie. In the meantime, it's an early night for both of us. Up with the lark to set sail from Fishguard.'

'It feels wicked. Going on holiday, seeing as how it will be washing day and everything.'

'Enjoy it, Maisie. It won't last long.'

It lasted one day and one night. Maisie never went on holiday, because she was snatched up like a criminal and and taken to the police station so fast she thought she might have dreamed Crawley's offer of a trip on a boat. But she didn't dream her mother's screams at the police station.

'You are a whore!'

'What, me, Mam?'

Maisie was stunned. She was poleaxed a second time in the interview room when she was shown a newspaper's front page story. It announced the arrest of two people for the murder of Myrtle Hughes.

'The alleged murderer and his teenage paramour were going to make their escape by ship . . .'

She pleaded her innocence.

'I never did nothing, sirs. Nothing.'

The shame of it all, though; all the disappointment, all the confusion. His sleepy, hot hands still against her calico-white skin, his lips wet on her stomach. Her burning face the colour of a stolen apple. But Crawley Hughes had never made her lie down with him. Maisie wanted so much to tell people that. But they wanted to believe in the callous daring of the murderer, who had dismembered his wife in the cellar as his 'paramour' cooked his tea in the kitchen above him. But he had sent her away on false missions. He had let her abandon him.

Maisie struggled with the truth, like she struggled with her aroused body, alone in a cell, lying on a plank of wood the width of the box room bed. She bent over her stomach in the night and kissed it with all the passion she had been denied when the police sealed a pair of handcuffs around her wrists. She had been torn from Crawley's side, clutching him so hard, her fingers had buried into the flesh on his shoulders. He had stood, dignified and very still, as she was carried away, screaming and biting at the strange hands which pawed at her twisting body. She screamed again when they said she was free to go. They admitted she was not an accessory to murder.

Two weeks after her dramatic arrest, Maisie left Holloway prison with Crawley Hughes' pocket watch wrapped up in a brown-paper parcel. He had sent it to her the day before he died on the gallows. Maisie decided to keep it. She would make a new season begin with just a twist of her fingers.

Acknowledgements

'Egg Spells' was originally published in 1997 in IOS New Short Stories (Independent on Sunday/ Bloomsbury). 'Kissing Calico' first appeared in Wild Cards (Virago, 1999). A version of 'Salt & Blood' was first published in Mslexia (2001) and also in New Welsh Review (No. 52). 'Playing the Joker' was first published in the anthology 'Her Majesty' (Tindal Street Press, 2002) and 'Dog Days' in New Welsh Review (No. 58).

When the Germans gained the upper hand in the Second World War and occupied what was then the United Kingdom, Hitler decided to make a very special case of Wales. New Wales – Cymru Newydd – was to be a special enclave for the Welsh people, a cruel demonstration of Nazi enlightenment, for it was intended to be nothing more than a labour camp – and a temporary one at that. As it happened, the vengeful vision of a ruthless dictator seemed to Dr Parry-Morris of Jesus College, Oxford, the opportunity for a great blossoming of Welsh culture and identity. For him, merely uttering the words 'Henffych Hitler' would be a very small price to pay for the prospects offered to his beloved Homeland. The scene was set for a seemingly stuffy old don to become Our First Leader, and lead Hitler a merry dance . . . This mischievous political satire from award-winning travel writer and Booker-shortlisted novelist Jan Morris should be compulsory reading for politicians everywhere.

'A fine piece of comic writing.' – *The Spectator*

ISBN 1 85902 852 7   £5.95